BOY BAND
OF THE APOCALYPSE
WASHED UP

FOR KATE, MY WONDERFUL MUM/MAM-IN-LAW – *TN*

FOR CHRIS & EMMA – *DO'C*

First American Edition 2019
Kane Miller, A Division of EDC Publishing

Text copyright © Tom Nicoll, 2018
Illustrations copyright © David O'Connell, 2018
Author photograph © Chris Scott
Illustrator photograph © Paul Galbraith
Images © shutterstock.com
First published in Great Britain in 2018 by STRIPES Publishing,
an imprint of the Little Tiger Group.

For information contact:
Kane Miller, A Division of EDC Publishing
PO Box 470663
Tulsa, OK 74147-0663
www.kanemiller.com
www.edcpub.com
www.usbornebooksandmore.com

Library of Congress Control Number: 2018942391

Printed and bound in the United States of America

1 2 3 4 5 6 7 8 9 10

ISBN: 978-1-61067-831-5

BOY BAND
OF THE APOCALYPSE
WASHED UP

TOM NICOLL

ILLUSTRATED BY
DAVID O'CONNELL

Kane Miller
A DIVISION OF EDC PUBLISHING

HYDE PARK: THE TRAGIC TRUTH

"What we saw was a publicity stunt gone wrong," revealed a government official, following an investigation into what has become known as the Hyde Park Incident. "There are NO Four Horsewomen of the Apocalypse. It was an elaborate stage show that ended tragically, costing the lives of the five beloved young men known as Apocalips."

Flying horses!!! Lol yeah, that's believable!!! @chrisdean

PUBLICITY STUNT? I was there that day, I saw what happened. Those girls were riding horses across the sky! @tiab01

SAMMY PARADE CALLED OFF

Plans for a parade in honor of Hyde Park "hero" Sam Miller were shelved yesterday following the public backlash leveled at Miller over his alleged involvement in the Hyde Park Incident. Outraged fans of deceased boy band Apocalips have been venting their fury online at the controversial "sixth" member who they claim has used the tragic events of that day to hoodwink people into believing he saved the world from total destruction. "He's just a no-talent ingrate," declared Paula Bradshaw, 15.

GOVERNMENT DENIES EXISTENCE OF APOCALYPSE INTELLIGENCE AGENCY

"There's absolutely no truth to these rumors," said the prime minister yesterday.

NEW ISLAND DISCOVERED IN BERMUDA TRIANGLE

Faulty satellites are to blame for not picking up the island until now, claimed a government official. Residents in nearby Puerto Rico have already nicknamed the new discovery *Fin Del Mundo* – Spanish for "End of the World."

CRUUL IN THE CLEAR

Nigel Cruul will not face charges over his involvement in the Hyde Park Incident, it was revealed yesterday, following a several-months-long investigation by the Metropolitan Police. Speaking outside his home, Cruul told reporters: "I am glad that finally the truth has come out. What happened at Hyde Park was a tragedy and

CRUUL SUMMER

Nigel Cruul was announced yesterday as the latest star to join the new reality TV show *End Games*. Cruul will join a host of celebrities in what is being described as a reality show unlike anything seen before. In something of a coup, the producers have landed exclusive access to the newly discovered island of Fin Del Mundo.

Aftermath: The Hottest New Band in Pop

"It's time to put the Hyde Park Incident in the past." EXCLUSIVE interview with Milo inside!

RUMOR: AFTER AFTERMATH IS MILO ABOUT TO GO SOLO?

Buzz continues to grow that Milo is about to make a MAJOR announcement about his future. But is he really about to DITCH his bandmates and strike out on his own?

Milo can sing, he can dance, he's cute and has a working knowledge of thermodynamics and quantum physics. What more could you want? @sumaya_g

OMG I LOVE MILO! HE'S MY ABSOLUTE FAVORITE MEMBER OF AFTERMATH. MARRY ME PLZ! @jessp99

JUDO'NT STAND A CHANCE!

Lexi Miller wiped the floor with her opponents last night to qualify for the Judo World Championships next summer. The athlete, 11, is also tipped to represent her country in karate and tae kwon do at the next Olympics.

CHAPTER ONE

AIA APOCALYPSE INTELLIGENCE AGENCY

I was on a plane. Not that I could see anything. A blindfold was covering my eyes. But between the roar of the engine, the smell of stale air and the overwhelming desire for my ears to pop, a bit of cloth wrapped around my head wasn't enough to disguise the fact I was airborne.

But ... *how* exactly?

The last thing I remembered was walking home from the corner shop with fish and chips for dinner. Mom and Dad are off touring with Aftermath – the band they manage – so my sister, Lexi, and I are staying with Gran for a few weeks. Not that I see much of Lexi these days. She's always at practice and… Actually, that's not that important right now. What's really important is that **I'M ON AN AIRPLANE!**

I tried to think. I had this vague memory of a black van pulling up alongside me and then… Well, I couldn't remember.

I attempted to lift my hands to take off the blindfold, then realized they were strapped to the armrests.

"Hello?" I said.

"Sam? Is that you?"

"Milo?" I cried, relieved to hear my best friend's voice, even though it didn't make the situation any less confusing. "What's going on?"

"No idea," he said. "One minute I'm heading back from the bathroom to join the guys for an interview in Dublin, the next I wake up blindfolded on a plane with you."

"And me."

"Lexi?" Milo and I said in unison.

"Did… Did you say we're on a plane?" asked my sister, her voice trembling a little.

"That's right," said Milo.

My sister is probably the bravest person I know. Except when it comes to planes. "Just breathe, Lexi," I said, trying to sound reassuring. "We're perfectly safe."

"And what part of us being abducted, blindfolded and stuck on a plane makes you think that exactly?" she asked.

She had a point. Before I had time to think of a reply, I heard what sounded like a door opening.

"Finally, they're awake," said a woman's voice. "All right, get those blindfolds and straps off and let's get started. We haven't got much time."

I heard footsteps as someone walked toward us. The next moment, the straps around my wrists were undone, and the blindfold was removed. I winced as light flooded my eyeballs. After about ten seconds of furious blinking, I could see we were sitting in cream leather seats in what looked like a private jet. In the aisle stood a man and a woman in black suits and dark glasses. The man was carrying a silver briefcase and was huge, a cross between a pro-wrestler and an even bigger pro-wrestler. Exactly the sort of person capable of grabbing someone off the street and bundling them into a van.

Yet somehow it was the woman half his size who seemed the more intimidating of the two. Her skin was pale, and her black hair was tied up in a bun so tight it threatened to snap her forehead.

"Relax, everyone," she said, with a thin smile. "No one's going to hurt you."

"Who are you?" I said. "What do you want?"

"My name is Special Agent Angela Banks," she said, holding out an ID card stamped with the letters **AIA**. "And this is my partner, Gary Speed. We're with the Apocalypse Intelligence Agency."

Milo let out a snort. "You mean the agency that doesn't exist?"

"Precisely," said Agent Banks. "The **AIA** was set up immediately after the Hyde Park Incident. The government realized they had been caught napping. If it hadn't been for the actions of a thirteen-year-old boy the entire planet would have been destroyed. A new top secret division was created with two goals – to shield the world from the truth of what happened that day, and to prevent it from ever happening again."

"To shield the world from the truth…" I repeated, realizing what she had just said. "So I'm guessing it was you who covered the whole thing up? Who made me out to be a liar?"

"Yes," she said calmly. "Understand, Sam, that the public are not best equipped to deal with the knowledge that they stand on the brink of destruction at any moment."

"They seemed to handle it fine from what I saw," I snapped.

Agent Banks shot me a withering smile. "We're very sorry you didn't get your parade, Mr. Miller, but sometimes tough decisions have to be made for the greater good. Which brings me to why you're here. We have reason to believe that a plot is under way to bring back the Horsewomen."

For a few seconds, the sound of the aircraft seemed to die away. Milo, Lexi and I looked at each other, the same shocked expression on our faces.

"But… But they're gone," said Lexi, the news appearing to make her forget that she was stuck in a tin can hurtling through the sky, at least for the moment.

"We fear not," put in Agent Speed. "Ever since the events at Hyde Park, our agency has been closely monitoring all kinds of unusual phenomena. I take it you've heard of Fin Del Mundo."

"Who's he?" I asked.

"It's not a who," said Milo. "It's a where. It's that island that's been all over the news."

"I've been trying to avoid the news," I admitted. "After all those stories about me being a fraud and then Cruul getting off… I got off social media, and I even got my hair put back the way it used to be. I just wanted things to return to normal."

11

Milo smiled awkwardly at this.

"Oh, I don't mean normal for you," I said quickly. "I mean obviously *you* don't want to go back to a normal boring life – you're, like, a superstar now. Everybody loves you. I meant normal for me." For some reason this didn't seem to help with the awkwardness between us.

"We're a long way from normal," said Agent Banks. She clicked her fingers, and Agent Speed opened his briefcase. He took out two glossy pictures and handed them to me.

"These haven't been released to the public," Banks continued. "The top image was taken four months ago from one of our satellites."

The picture in question didn't show an awful lot – just water.

"Now look at the second picture," she said. "The exact same location, three weeks later."

The second picture was of a jungle-covered island with a mountain in the middle.

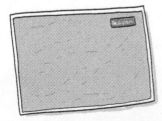 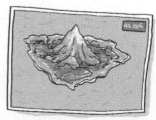

"You're looking at Fin Del Mundo," Agent Banks said. "The planet's newest island."

"I don't understand," I said. "How—"

"The reason Fin Del Mundo hasn't been discovered until now is because it wasn't there," she interrupted.

"That's pretty weird," I admitted.

"That's not all," she said. I'd thought it probably wasn't. "Ever heard of the Bermuda Triangle?"

"Sure," said Milo. "Also known as the Devil's Triangle. Lying in the North Atlantic Ocean between Florida, Puerto Rico and Bermuda, it's famous for planes and boats mysteriously disappearing inside it."

Agent Banks nodded. "Exactly. Things tend to go missing there. They don't usually get found. Especially not entire islands like this one."

"Actually, it's been a while since anything went missing there," noted Agent Speed, reaching into his briefcase and handing me a sheet of paper. On it was a chart.

13

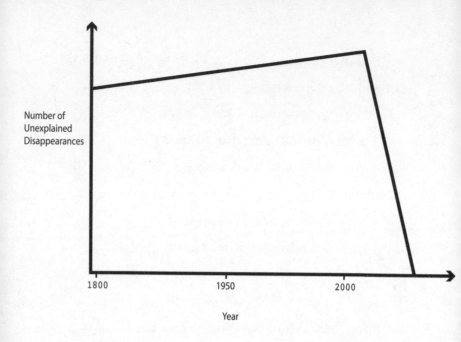

Number of Unexplained Disappearances

1800   1950   2000

Year

"Why does it drop off after the year 2000?" I said.

"2004, to be exact," said Agent Speed. "There could be any number of reasons. Improvements in communications devices, better-designed vehicles. Even changes to flight plans and trading routes might be responsible."

I could tell from the looks the agents were exchanging that neither of them believed those theories. "What do you think really happened?" I asked.

14

"There's something particularly significant about that year," said Agent Banks. "It was when you were born."

I couldn't help but laugh. "That's your theory?" I said. "That baby me helped improve safety in the Bermuda Triangle?"

"Not directly," said Agent Banks. "But we do know that the Horsewomen took great interest in your birth. They monitored you closely, infiltrating your life early on at school as the Heatherstones. From that point on, their focus was on you and their, admittedly justified, fears that you might be the one to thwart their plans to finally bring about the Apocalypse."

"OK, but what's that got to do with the Bermuda Triangle?" said Lexi.

"We're not sure exactly," admitted Agent Speed. "We might have assumed the timing was purely coincidental. But given the sudden appearance of the island and the fact that Nigel Cruul is on his way out there … well, we're not so certain."

"You think Cruul's up to something?" said Milo.

Agent Banks nodded. "Oh, Cruul is always up to something," she said. "Our concern is whether that something involves bringing back the Four Horsewomen of the Apocalypse. He was the Horsewomen's right-hand man. We can't ignore the possibility that they may have left him instructions in the event of their demise. A Plan B so to speak."

"Hang on," I said. "Cruul's on his way to Fin Del Mundo?"

"You didn't know that?" said Lexi. "He's taking part in that new reality TV show **End Games** with some other minor celebrities, doing silly challenges on a desert island."

"It's been all over the news," said Milo.

I shrugged. "You know I don't follow the news these days," I said. Then something troubling occurred to me. "Wait a second ... where do *we* fit into this?"

Agent Banks grinned. "That reality show? We're sending you three on it too."

CHAPTER TWO

APOCALYPSE INTELLIGENCE AGENCY

I shook my head. "No. No. No. No. No. No," I said, then in case I hadn't made myself clear: "**NO!**"

"But—" said Agent Banks.

"No!" I repeated. "You can't just go around abducting people and then expecting them to go on reality TV shows for you."

"We're the government," she replied. "I think you'll find we can."

Agent Speed shifted nervously. "Actually, boss, he's right. We're not really allowed to abduct people anymore. We're especially not meant to drug them and fly them out of the country."

Agent Banks screwed up her face. "No abductions? Seriously? Since when?"

"Well, according to Simmonds in Analysis, we've never been allowed to abduct people," he said matter-of-factly. "It's just that we've seen it happen in the movies and think we can do it in real life."

"But it's the best part of the job," she said, pouting slightly before remembering we were there. "Anyway, we're talking about the greater good here. The fate of the world could be at stake. What's a few abductions in the grand scheme of things?"

I shook my head. Just the thought of being back in the public eye made me feel queasy. "Like I told you, I'm not going on a celebrity TV show," I said. "I'm not a celebrity. Now get me out of here."

"But you're perfect," said Agent Banks. "You're experienced in undercover missions. You know Cruul as well as anyone. We think your presence alone might be enough to put him on edge, to cause him to make mistakes."

"Can't you just send some agents to the island?" I asked. "You know, people who are actually

18

trained in this stuff?"

Agent Banks shook her head. "We need someone who can get close to Cruul. That means we need someone on the show. And the show wants celebrities. We'd hardly be able to get a government agent on the show, would we?"

That did seem a bit unlikely.

"But I'm not even a real celebrity," I said.

Agents Banks and Speed started laughing. "You haven't watched much reality TV, have you?" said Speed.

"Trust us," said Banks, "compared to some, you're overqualified. The truth is, you're exactly the kind of person who'd go on a show like this. Most of the contestants are washed-up stars hoping to make a comeback. No one would be surprised to see a former boy band member desperately trying to claw his way back into the limelight."

"And this is really just a reconnaissance mission," said Agent Speed. "You three just need to find out Cruul's plans for the Horsewomen, report back to us, and we'll handle the rest."

I knew enough about trying to save the world to know that things were never so simple. "What if I don't," I said. "And he manages to bring them back?"

"Well, at least you'll be nearby when it happens," said Agent Banks.

"Oh, great," I groaned.

Agent Banks smiled. "What I meant was, if it happens, you can just sing at them again, can't you?"

So basically I was a busker assassin. Then something else occurred to me, and I felt my blood start to boil again.

"If it weren't for you guys lying about what happened at Hyde Park then none of this would be necessary," I said. "Cruul would be in prison, and you'd never have to worry about him bringing the Horsewomen back."

"On the contrary," said Agent Banks. "If Cruul hadn't gone free then we'd have zero leads on how to stop the Horsewomen. You think Cruul is the only Apocalyte out there? We seriously doubt that. There's no telling how wide their network is. If it wasn't Cruul doing the Horsewomen's dirty work then it'd be someone else – maybe a movie star or a celebrity chef. It could be anyone who owes their success to them and wants to step up to prove their devotion. We're lucky in that at least we know our enemy. We can't do this without you, Sam."

I turned to Milo for backup, but I could tell from his face I wasn't going to get it. "What?" I asked him wearily.

"I think we have to," he said. "It's like she says, we're talking about the fate of the world. And we stopped them before. Who better than us to stop them again?"

"What about your tour?" I said.

"It can wait," he said. "This is more important."

I could feel the tide turning against me. "What about you, Lexi?"

"Huh?" said Lexi. "Sorry, what were you guys saying?" Her face was white as she gripped the armrests with all her might. Clearly her focus was back on her fear of flying.

"They want to send us on a reality TV show to

find out what Cruul's up to," I said. "What do you think?"

"Will it get us off this plane?" she asked.

"Well, yes, but what about your training and—"

"I'm in," said Lexi.

"Excellent. It's all been arranged," Banks said. "The producers were falling over themselves when we offered Milo. And Lexi was an easy sell too, what with that video of her beating up the Horsewomen going viral before we released the hoax story. And then there's the dynamic of the three of you being on the same show as Nigel Cruul. No TV producer is going to pass up the chance for sparks to fly—"

"So you'd already set this up," I interrupted. "Before we even said yes?"

Banks didn't even blink. "We had to move fast. And we had faith that you would do what's right. So yes, we got the ball rolling. We had your luggage packed, and agents have been in contact with your parents and grandmother to explain the situation. We even had your hair done."

I ran a hand through my hair. "Ow!"

Banks pulled out a hand mirror from her pocket and held it up. My head looked like someone had stuck a blond porcupine to it. It was the same haircut I had sported during my time in Apocalips.

"H-how?" I stammered. "W-why?"

"We had it done en route to the plane," she explained. "When you were asleep. How else are people going to recognize you if you don't have your boy band haircut?"

I gave a long sigh.

"OK," said Agent Banks, looking at her watch. "I'm going to go check with the pilot, see how we're doing. Agent Speed will run you through your initiation."

As she headed back up to the cockpit, Agent Speed did a little cough to clear his throat. "Right. **AIA** protocol states that all persons engaging in undercover operations on behalf of the agency will be subject to intensive and exhaustive training beforehand. This will help prepare them for any issues they may encounter in the field to maximize chances of a successful operation. Normally this could take anywhere from six months to a year, but we're going to have to cut that down a bit."

"How long have we got?" asked Milo.

Agent Speed checked his watch. "About ten minutes."

CHAPTER THREE

"Ten minutes?" I repeated, regretting my decision. "What exactly are we going to learn in ten minutes?"

"Well, I thought we might go over how you guys will communicate with us," Agent Speed said, taking some sheets of paper out of his briefcase. "Obviously, you won't be able to pick up a phone, so we'll have to be a bit smarter. We can take advantage of the fact that this is a reality TV show. There may be opportunities for you to send coded messages to us. I've drawn up a guide of some examples that you should be able to slip seamlessly into the show without raising any suspicions."

We looked at the guide.

CODE	MESSAGE
Is it just me or does that coconut look a bit like the prime minister?	Cruul is definitely here to bring about the return of the Four Horsewomen of the Apocalypse.
Is it just me or does that coconut look a bit like the queen?	Cruul's plan is almost complete.
Is it just me or does that coconut look a bit like Taylor Swift?	Our lives are in danger. Send help immediately.
Is it just me or does that coconut look a bit like Wayne Rooney?	Everything's fine.

The list went on like that for several pages. "It's quite coconut based," observed Lexi.

"Yes!" Agent Speed nodded enthusiastically. "I was up all night working on it."

"What do we do if there isn't a coconut nearby?" asked Milo.

Agent Speed opened his mouth to speak, then shut it. "Oh," he said. "I hadn't thought about that. I'm sure you'll figure it out."

Milo rolled his eyes. "Maybe we should go over something useful," he said. "Like the Horsewomen themselves. I've been researching them during my downtime on the tour bus."

"You've actually found stuff on the Horsewomen?" I asked, impressed. I had tried googling them once or twice, but all I had managed to find was random articles on cowgirls, centaurs and jockeys. I suspected Milo's research techniques were a bit more sophisticated.

"I think so," he said. "It's not been easy, though. It's not like they've got Wikipedia pages or Facebook profiles. You have to look between the lines of history to find them, but they're definitely there. Especially whenever things went drastically wrong. And each seems to represent their own corner of misery and suffering: Death, War, Famine and Pestilence."

"The stuff they put on plants to keep bugs off?" I asked.

"That's pesticides," said Milo. "Pestilence is a massively deadly disease, like the bubonic plague."

Suddenly things started sliding into place.

"Wait a minute," I said. "Veronica was Donnie in Apocalips. She had that booming voice and dressed in black. So she was ... or is ... Death?"

"Yup," said Milo, grinning. "And the others?"

"Well, Vicky was always the most aggressive of the four," I said. "And she was Warren in Apocalips... Wow, she didn't even bother trying with that name, did she? She's War."

"Two for two," said Milo.

"Violet was Frankie," I said. "And I never once saw Frankie eat anything. So I'm guessing Violet is Famine."

"Leaving Valerie as Pete, so she must be Pesticides," said Lexi triumphantly.

"Pestilence," corrected Milo.

"Whatever," said Lexi. "The point is they're all massive jerks."

"Interesting," I said, turning back to Agent Speed. "So what is it we're supposed to do when we get to the island? If Cruul's up to something, he's not going to just tell us, is he?"

"Our theory is that the island itself holds the

key," said Agent Speed. "That's got to be why he's heading out there. You're going to have to explore the place and discover its secrets."

"And just how are we meant to do that," I asked, "with cameras filming our every move? You're dropping us in with no notice and no training… I mean, isn't there anything useful you can give us?"

Agent Speed scratched his chin for a few seconds before slapping his forehead. "Of course!" he cried. "Why didn't I think of this earlier?"

He reached into his briefcase and removed what looked like a small battery. "I just got this from O'Brien, one of our engineering techs. I was supposed to give it to Agent Banks, but given the circumstances, I clean forgot. I doubt she'd mind you having it, though. They call it a Time-Out. Press this little button on the top, and it'll send out a short-range, low-power electromagnetic pulse, strong enough to temporarily disable any electronic device within a fifty-foot radius. Its effects will only last a couple of minutes, tops, but that should be enough to help with getting past cameras or buying yourself some time to speak to each other privately."

Finally, something that might actually be useful. I could still see one problem, though. "How am I going to smuggle this on to the show?" I asked.

"Easy," said Agent Speed, taking out a roll of scarlet tape. He tore off a strip and wrapped it around the device. "This is government red tape – it retains its stick for years. Nothing will shift it."

He leaned over and buried the Time-Out deep in my hair. I raised my hand to touch it only to have Lexi grab my wrist.

"Don't you dare do that in here," she warned. "As if it wasn't bad enough flying into the Bermuda Triangle, you could disable this plane with the press of a button."

"Sorry," I said.

Agent Speed checked his watch, then took out some more sheets of paper from his briefcase. "Now there's just enough time to run through the other contestants. We've put together profiles on each of them."

"These look like cutouts from a newspaper," said Lexi as Speed handed us each a copy.

"All right, fine," grumbled Speed. "We didn't have time for that so we just photocopied a pullout from the *Daily Blowhorn*."

"Look, Betty Black's in it," said Lexi.

For almost fifty years, Betty Black has graced our television screens as pub landlady and reformed jewel thief Norma Braithwaite in the country's most popular soap opera, *Cliffhanger Road*. She broke  viewers' hearts last Christmas when she finally bowed out of the show in typical Norma style, throwing herself on a grenade hidden inside a Christmas pudding to save the lives of everyone in the Kings Legs pub. Betty, 72, is ready for a new adventure on Fin Del Mundo. Let's just hope that all those years of playing streetwise Norma come in handy for this National Treasure.

"Mom loves that show," said Milo. "She cried for ages when Norma died. Oh, they've got that vlogger guy Bo, too."

"Bo?" asked Lexi. "Bo what?"

"Just Bo," said Milo.

Vlogger, e-sports megastar, entrepreneur and now … survivalist? Bo, the self-proclaimed King of the Internet, has created his own online empire. His videos, released almost hourly, average 100 million views each, and his video explaining how to build a combine harvester in Minecraft has been watched over three billion times. Known for his enthusiasm and constant perkiness, the big question is, will Bo manage to remain upbeat when he realizes that there's no Wi-Fi on the island?

"Right, yeah, I think I've watched one of his videos," I said. "He literally spent the entire time comparing apples and oranges—"

"Ooh, Joe Bruiser's on this as well!" interrupted Lexi.

"Who's Joe Bruiser?" asked Milo. "Wait … not that balding guy who's always calling everyone a mug?"

"That's the one," I said.

"He's only, like, one of the toughest guys in the country," said Lexi. "And he only calls people mugs if they're being mugs. And he's not balding. Well, not much. What does it say about him?"

Raised on the mean streets of East London, or "Lahndon" as he calls it, Joe Bruiser, born Joseph Bruisington, has carved out a career playing the tough guy with a heart of gold  in such films as *Look Who's Cockney*, *Avin' a Laff* and *You Silly Mug!* Never shy of conflict, it'll be interesting to see how Joe gets on with some of the more difficult contestants. Will there be Barney Rubble (trouble) or will everyone be china plates (mates)? Watch and find out!

"I've seen every film he's ever made," said Lexi. "Even the terrible ones like Soccer Heroes and Soccer Heroes Eight."

Milo and I looked at each other. "What about Soccer Heroes two to seven?" I asked.

"They were all right," she said, turning the page. "Ooh, what a surprise, Zizi Summer is on this thing too."

This was the first name I didn't recognize. I glanced at her picture – a young, glossy-haired girl, pouting at the camera – then turned to Milo.

"You must have seen her, she's everywhere," he said. "She's at all the award shows and parties we go to. And she's always in the papers."

"What does she do?"

Milo shrugged. "Nothing really," he said. "She just kind of does this."

"What do you mean 'this'?" I asked.

"Shows like this," he said. "She's been on

everything. The Only Way is West Sussex, Celebrity Caravanning, Celebrity Board Game World Cup. And she had those shows where they just followed her around in different seasons – *Summer in Spring, Summer in Summer, Summer in Autumn* and … there was another one, but I forget what it was called."

We both laughed.

"She's the one that thought Brussels sprouts were just moldy potatoes," said Lexi, glancing out of the window for a second before quickly turning away again.

"That's her," said Milo. "And she once got an airport shut down when she tried to bring her dogs on the plane with her."

I pictured a couple of fluffy little dogs, small enough to fit inside a handbag.

As if reading my thoughts, Milo shook his head. "There were fifty of them," he said. "It was for a show she was doing where celebrities ran a dog kennel. After the series finished, she wanted to treat all the dogs to a fortnight in the Seychelles."

"Yikes," I said.

We quickly flicked through the profiles on Cruul, Lexi and Milo, given that we knew everything about them already. Lastly there was a bit on the hosts Ronald and Donald, two men with the faces of a couple of twelve-year-olds and the receding hairlines of guys in their forties. Sometimes it felt like they presented every show on television. Despite this, most people could never remember which one was which, even though Ronald is about a head taller with black hair, and Donald has blond hair and big ears.

One profile was noticeably absent. "Where's mine?" I asked.

Agent Speed looked away. "Oh, is it not in there? I thought it was. It must have been a printing error…"

"It's in my copy," said Lexi.

"It is?" said Agent Speed, looking panicked. "It's not meant to be! Um … I mean … how odd…"

I snatched the page from Lexi before Speed could get to it. "Why don't you want me to read it? Oh."

The answer to the trivia question, who was the sixth member of Apocalips? Sam "Sammy" Miller went from hero to zero when the truth was finally revealed about the  tragic circumstances at Hyde Park last year where the beloved boy band came to an untimely end. Miller, 14, had us all convinced that he had saved the world, when in fact the only person he saved was himself. Not a day goes by where we don't wonder why a nobody like Miller was spared at the expense of five of the most talented young men this planet has ever known. So can the massive liar Sam master the skills required to survive on the island or… Ah, who cares? Hopefully he'll get eaten by something horrible or his parachute won't open. Sam stinks!

I glanced up. "They don't like me, do they?"

Agent Speed looked apologetic. "I really wouldn't take much notice."

"Yeah, who cares what that rag says," offered Milo.

"It's easy for you to say," I muttered. "You were up there onstage with the Horsewomen too, but no one accuses *you* of being a fraud. You got a pop career out of it. I'm the one everyone hates. What is it you said in that magazine again? You want to 'distance' yourself from what happened."

Milo looked a little taken aback at my outburst. "I didn't want to," he said quietly. "The band thought it best…"

I was about to reply when something caught my eye. Where there had once been blue ocean merging seamlessly into blue sky, something else had finally come into view through the window next to Lexi. Land.

Milo and I rushed to the other side of the plane to get a better look. Beneath us the greenest trees and plants sprawled out across a large lemon-shaped island, occasionally crisscrossed by bright-blue rivers and ringed by yellow sandy beaches. As the plane began to circle, we could see the centerpiece of it all – a mountain that seemed to grasp desperately at the sky itself.

"I didn't think it would be so big," I said.

"Me neither," said Milo.

"Sorry," I said. "I didn't mean to go off at you there. It's just reading all those things about me—"

"Hey, what did it mean by 'parachute'?" interrupted Lexi.

"Parachute?" repeated Milo, still gazing out of the window.

"In Sam's profile," she went on. "It said they hoped his parachute didn't open. What parachute?"

The three of us turned to Agent Speed, who was smiling sheepishly.

The door to the cockpit burst open and Agent Banks emerged, carrying three large backpacks.

"I'm going to guess," said Milo, "that they were talking about those things."

CHAPTER FOUR

"All up to speed, Speed?" asked Agent Banks as she shoved a backpack into my hands.

"Er ... yes, boss," said Agent Speed, rubbing the back of his neck. "I think the parachutes might have come as a surprise, though."

"We ... don't ... really have ... to jump ... out of this ... thing, do we?" asked Lexi.

Agent Banks screwed up her face. "How else did you think you were getting off?"

"By landing?" suggested Milo, pointing toward the island. "Look, there's a whole field down there that would be perfect for an airstrip."

"This is TV," she said. "Who wants to watch

that? The production company were happy for us to arrange for you to get to the island, given the last-minute nature of everything. But our instructions were to drop you off. Literally."

"Don't you need training before you can make a parachute jump?" I asked.

Agent Banks nodded. "Normally."

Normally. Just like normally you'd be given training before going on an undercover mission. But, as Agent Banks said, we were a long way from normal.

"Don't worry, these are state-of-the-art parachutes," she said. "They're designed to open automatically. All you need to do is make sure you're strapped in. And then jump, obviously."

"What about our luggage?" I asked. "You said you'd brought it."

"I just jettisoned it a minute ago," she said. "The crew from the show will collect it. Now you three better get moving. Agent Speed will fit you with headcams so that the viewers can see what you see on the way down and mic packs so—"

"They can hear our screams?" interrupted Lexi.

I grabbed hold of my sister's arms. "It'll be OK," I said, trying to convince myself as much as her. I had never really had to reassure Lexi about anything before. It felt wrong, like being asked to help Milo with his homework.

Milo had already strapped on his backpack. Inside, I didn't feel any more enthusiastic than Lexi, but I knew I had to put on a brave face, or she'd never agree to do it. I slipped on mine as Agent Speed attached the headcam and mic pack. It was just Lexi to convince now. The fact that she had curled herself up in a ball was not encouraging.

"No chance!" she said.

I looked to Milo for help. After a few moments he held a finger in the air.

"Lexi," he said. "You don't like flying, do you?"

My sister shot him a look.

"What I mean," said Milo, pressing on, "is that if you don't like flying, then it's a strange decision not to jump. You've been flying for about eight hours. If you don't come with us, you'll have to stay on this plane all the way back home."

Lexi sat up. "But I'll still have to fly home," she said. "Once the show's over."

"Maybe, or maybe we can convince them to send out a boat or something," said Milo.

"A boat?" she said. "Do you think they might?"

"Sure," said Milo. He looked to Agent Banks for support.

"Um… Yes, definitely," she said. "They could get one of those cruise ships to pick you up."

I could tell by the way Lexi's eyes were flickering back and forth that she was desperate to believe it.

"That's right," said Milo. "So the only way I can see for you to never be in the air again is to jump."

A wide-eyed Lexi turned to me then back to Milo. After a moment or two of weighing up the options, she suddenly hopped out of her seat, slung a backpack over her shoulders and strapped herself in.

"That's great, Lexi," I said. "We'll help each other… Lexi?"

But she wasn't listening. She was too busy opening the plane door.

"Er… Lexi?" said Milo, but his voice was drowned out by the noise as the air whooshed in. Then Lexi was gone.

Milo and I stared through the door open-mouthed as Lexi plummeted earthward.

"To be honest, I didn't think I'd be that convincing!" shouted Milo.

"You can be very persuasive!" I screamed back. After all, he had managed to convince me to risk my life attempting to save the world. Twice.

We continued to watch Lexi fall. Then her parachute opened like a bright-red flower.

"Thank goodness for that." I sighed.

Milo looked just as relieved. "Well … shall we?"

"You first," I said.

"No, no, be my guest," said Milo.

"Please, after you," I said.

It was at that point that Agent Banks leaned over and shoved Milo out of the plane.

"Hey!" I shouted.

"Sorry, but we really don't have time for this," she said. She raised her arm toward me.

"I can do it myself," I said. I turned and peered out of the door. It was a long way down. I looked back at Agent Banks. "Actually, if you wouldn't mind?"

"Good luck," she said, giving me a shove.

Falling from that height feels a lot like flying. Though it's probably important that you don't confuse the two. As I spiraled through the air, the island zooming toward me, I caught sight of Milo some way below me just as his chute opened.

Seconds passed, but mine still hadn't. My brain used the opportunity to start thinking up what-if scenarios. Like:

What if I was so hated that someone *had* tampered with my parachute?

What if they'd mixed up my luggage bag with my parachute bag, and I was now going to have to try to land using my underwear?

What if when it opened, an anvil came flying out like it always did in old cartoons?

I could feel myself breaking out in a cold sweat. Just as I was convinced I was a goner, my parachute burst open, and I felt my speed drop. I scanned the ground below for a safe landing spot.

I could see palm trees, sand, more palm trees, some sand, palm trees again, even more sand, a giant black skull, palm trees…

Yeah, it was probably the giant black skull, wasn't it? It was printed on a huge piece of canvas spread across the beach. As something to aim for it certainly stood out, but as a welcome sign it left a lot to be desired.

I tried my best to steer toward it, not really sure how. This was where training would have come in handy. But after several seconds of fumbling at my backpack I found two cords attached to either side. By pulling them I could make myself turn in a particular direction. Somehow I was able to keep myself on target as the skull got closer and closer.

I could see Lexi had already landed. Someone was helping her with her chute, but even from my height there was an unmistakable look of panic on her face. As my mind began to race, I almost forgot I was about to hit the ground.

I overshot the giant skull, tripped, and fell face-first onto the beach.

I sat up, spitting out a mouthful of sand. I suppose that could have gone worse. A guy with a camera was already hovering nearby, probably getting a good close-up.

Someone dragged me to my feet. "All right, sunshine?" said a short, heavily muscled man in a gruff voice. "You 'it that ground like a sack of potatoes."

"You're—" I said.

"Joe Bruiser, pleased to meet ya," he said as he helped untangle me from my chute.

"Lexi?" I said.

"You mean that kid over there?" he said. "She's fine. It's that other one you want to be worried about."

"You mean Milo?" I asked as the backpack that had held my chute fell to the ground. I hurried over to Lexi as people rushed past us toward the sea.

"What's happened?" I asked.

"It's Milo," she said. "He must have lost control. He landed in the water."

CHAPTER FIVE

Milo was a lot of things. He was an inventor and a singer and a superstar. But the one thing he wasn't was a swimmer. It wasn't so long ago that he was too afraid to even leave the house, let alone learn how to not die in a pool of water.

I could make out Milo's parachute bobbing on the waves but couldn't see him.

"Don't tell me he can't swim?" said an obnoxious-sounding voice to my right. I looked around to see a tall, tanned man in his early twenties shaking his head – Bo. He took off a pair of sunglasses and placed them on his coiffed hair. "Why'd he even come on a show like this, then?

There's always swimming on these things."

He came on the show to try to save the world, I wanted to shout. But there wasn't time to waste on this idiot. I had to rescue Milo.

I kicked off my shoes and was about to plunge into the sea when I felt Lexi's hand pulling me back.

"Look, someone's already got him," she said, pointing at the water.

Sure enough, I could just make out someone with Milo, the two of them heading toward shore. But my relief quickly turned to anger when I realized who it was. Cruul.

Suddenly they stopped.

"What are they doing?" I cried.

But then I saw. They weren't alone in the water. A single fin was heading straight for them.

"SHARK!" screamed Lexi.

Why weren't they moving? Cruul was behind Milo, using him as a shield. He was about to feed my best friend to a shark, and there was nothing I could do.

As the shark bore down on them, Milo's parachute suddenly came free. There was a **WHUMP** as the wind caught it, sending the chute exploding into the shark's face, propelling it backward.

A cheer went up across the beach.

"Cruul must have gotten Milo's parachute off," said Lexi.

They were certainly moving much faster through the water now. Moments later, Nigel Cruul strode onto the beach with a coughing and spluttering Milo in his arms.

I couldn't move at first, unable to grasp what

was happening. There could be only one explanation. Unless I had somehow parachuted into an alternative universe where Nigel Cruul, instead of being one of the most evil men alive, was actually a hero who had just saved my best friend, then something … well, fishy was going on.

"He's swallowed a bit of water," said Cruul as someone handed him a towel, which he used to dry his head and his bearlike hairy chest, "but luckily I got to him in time. He'll be fine."

I barged through the crowd and grabbed Milo by the arms. Instinctively I put myself between Milo and Cruul, before realizing it was entirely pointless. Whatever reasons Cruul had for rescuing Milo, it probably wasn't to then try and harm him right in front of a group of people. On national TV.

"Th-thank you," spluttered Milo, looking toward Cruul.

"Quite all right," said Cruul.

"Don't thank him," I said.

All heads turned toward me.

"Ah… Sammy," said Cruul wearily.

"SAM!" I shouted. "My name's Sam, not Sammy."

Cruul smiled. "Yes, of course," he said. "Old habits die hard."

"I'll bet," I said. "Why did you do that? Why did you save him?"

"I'm sorry," he said. "Would you rather I had left him out there?"

I could hear some of the people around me tittering.

"I know you, Cruul," I said. "You don't do anything if it's not in your interest."

"Says the boy who lied his way into a pop band," said Cruul. "Is it really so hard to believe that I saved Milo because I didn't want him to drown?"

"YES!" I shouted.

Cruul didn't reply. He just tilted his head and gave me this look of complete pity. It was the sort of withering gaze he used to give when he was judging talent shows.

That's when I became aware I was being watched. Not just by the other contestants. Among them were a man and woman, each holding a video camera, both of which were alternating between Cruul and me.

"You just saved him to look good on TV," I said.

Cruul made a pained expression. "You're so cynical," he said. "And even if I did, do you think I'm the only one here hoping to come across well on camera? To improve my image? Look around you. I can assure you I'm not alone."

"I hope you're not talking about me, young man," said a posh-sounding voice. It was Betty Black. It was weird hearing her talk like that, seeing as her character on Cliffhanger Road had an East London accent that put Joe Bruiser to shame. Given the perfect condition of her massive bouffant hairdo, it seemed a safe bet that she hadn't been asked to parachute in.

"Of course not, Betty," said Cruul. "Had much work since they wrote you out of the show?"

"How dare you…" said Betty, looking flustered.

"The fact is," said Cruul smugly, "the only person who doesn't stand to gain much from being on this show is the young man I just saved. Unlike everyone else –" he glanced at the rest of us – "his career is on the up. I can't really get my head around it, to be honest. Unless… Ah yes, of course. He must be here to help his best friend."

I gave Milo a nervous glance. Did Cruul already know we were here to stop his plans? "What do you mean?" Milo asked.

"What else *could* I mean?" he said. "You're hoping your popularity rubs off on him. Everyone knows Sammy's not very well liked. Still, if I were your manager, I wouldn't have let you come. This show's beneath you, Milo."

"Well, you're not his manager," I said.

"More's the pity," said Cruul. "When I think of all I could do with a band like Aftermath…"

I laughed at the thought. Aftermath was the

complete opposite of the groups Cruul managed. Its members were misfits – talented but unique individuals, not dull cookie-cutter clones. I was just about to point this out when a shadow briefly passed over us, accompanied by the roar of a plane flying overhead.

Everyone turned to see another parachute drifting over the beach, before touching down right in the center of the black skull. Whoever the new contestant was, it was clear they had done this before, from the way they quickly extracted themselves from their chute.

I looked around to see who we were missing. It could only be Zizi Summer.

She was sprinting toward us. Or rather, she was sprinting toward something else and *that* was sprinting toward us.

"Pierre, no!" she shouted, but it was no use. The fastest, most furious-looking pug I'd ever seen soared through the air and came crashing down on Nigel Cruul.

CHAPTER SIX

"Get that mutt off me!" shouted Cruul, writhing around on the sand as the pug growled and snapped at him.

"Pierre! Bad!" said Zizi, scooping up the pug and holding him to her face. "What a naughty doggy-woggy you are!"

"Naughty? That thing tried to kill me!" yelled Cruul, pulling himself up.

"Pierre wouldn't hurt a fly," said Zizi. "He just got a bit excited after his first parachute jump. Didn't you, snookie-wookums?" As if in agreement, Pierre started licking Zizi's lips, covering her face in drool.

"Eurgh, that's disgusting," muttered Bo.

"What's that dog even doing here?" asked Cruul.

"I don't go anywhere without my baby," said Zizi.

"Well, keep him away from me," said Cruul.
"I'm— **ACHOO!**"

"Sorry?" said Zizi. "You're what?"

"I think he was about to say he's allergic to dogs?"
I said, grinning.

Zizi looked bewildered by the thought. "Surely you
can't be allergic to Pierre?" she said. "He's a *nice* dog."

"**ACHOOOO!**" screamed Cruul, blowing a stream
of snot into the face of a woman who had just
arrived, clutching a tablet and a walkie-talkie.

"Ugh, perfect," she said, wiping it off. "All right, guys, my name's Karen. I'm the production manager. Now if everyone can please follow me, we're due to go live in a few minutes."

With Cruul trailing along at the back, still sniveling, we followed Karen up the beach, cameras filming our every step.

Finally we reached a cave. I stopped suddenly, causing Lexi to bang into me.

"Ow!" she moaned. "Why did you stop?"

"It was just… Sorry, it doesn't matter," I said, giving an involuntary shudder as I remembered the last time I had been in a cave. Of course, that one had been located in another dimension, and I had been a prisoner inside it. So not quite the same, but it still felt a little weird as I stepped into the gloom.

At the opposite end of a large chamber, a row of folding chairs faced a stage with a red velvet curtain drawn across it. Dark shadows danced across the drapes, caused by the flickering of the hundreds of candles that lined the walls.

"This is just like the set we used in the music video for Transylvania-Mania," said Milo.

"Very 'andy," said Joe Bruiser, pulling a cigar from the pocket of his shorts and using one of the candles to light it.

"You can't smoke that in here," protested Milo as Joe took several puffs, before returning the candle to its holder.

"Course I can," said Joe, giving him a big grin. "Until they figure out which country owns this place, there's no one to enforce a smokin' ban, is there?"

Milo opened his mouth to speak, then frowned.

"He's got you there," said Lexi.

Milo muttered something under his breath before heading off toward the opposite side of the cave. I sat down between him and Zizi. On the seat next to her was Pierre, who was busy licking his rear.

"This is exciting, eh?" said Zizi, giving me a gentle nudge. "Your first time on one of these shows, then?"

I nodded, glancing around for Lexi. She was sitting next to Bruiser and appeared to be badgering him with questions.

"Well, you're in for a treat," said Zizi. "I love doing them. I must have done about twenty last year. Twenty-one if you count the one I accidentally made myself when I left my laptop's webcam on for five months."

Zizi was cut off by the sound of rock music blasting out of the speakers on stage as the curtain dropped to reveal two men dressed in bright-orange Hawaiian shirts, khaki shorts and white sandals.

"*Aloha*," said Ronald.

"That's Hawaiian, you doofus!" Donald laughed.

"Well, where are we?" asked Ronald.

"We're on a mysterious island called Fin Del Mundo, in the center of the Bermuda Triangle," said Donald.

"Bermuda?" said Ronald. "At least we got the shorts right, then!"

Zizi burst out laughing. "**O-M-G**, those guys are too funny," she said, slapping her thighs.

"Well, Donald, why are we here?" asked Ronald.

"Because it's in our contracts," replied Donald.

"Fair enough," said Ronald. He waved his hands toward us. "So why are *they* here?"

"They're here to take part in the toughest, most grueling, most disgusting reality show ever produced!" said Donald.

"Sounds like fun," said Ronald.

"It's not!"

Then, in unison, the two of them shouted at the same camera: "**WELCOME TO END GAMES!**"

All the candles in the cave flickered.

"Are you guys ready to play?" asked Ronald.

There was a murmur among the contestants.

"He said, are you guys ready to play?" repeated Donald.

There was a slightly louder, more enthusiastic mumble of agreement. Except from Zizi, who stood up and screamed, "**WOOOOOOHOOOOO!**"

"That's a bit more like it," said Ronald. "OK, Donald, shall we explain the rules?"

"If we must," said Donald. "All right, here's what you need to know. Some of you who can count might have noticed that there's eight of you here, not including Pierre, of course. Unlike other shows, this isn't about individuals. This is a team game.

You're going to be split into two teams. Four against four. Your only aim is to make sure your team wins. The only prize will be the sweet taste of victory over your rivals."

Bruiser and Bo made grumbling noises at this.

"And five hundred thousand pounds…" added Ronald.

The grumbling turned to cheers.

"…to be given to a charity of your team's choice," finished Donald.

And back to grumbling.

"There will be a series of challenges," continued Ronald. "Now, there are two types of challenge – Elimination and Golden. An Elimination Challenge is exactly what it sounds like. If you lose, you're off the island. Every day, members of the public will vote for the person they want to see face the chop. The contestants on each team with the most votes will then face each other in a fiendish challenge, live in front of the nation." He turned to the camera, then added: "Voting for tomorrow's challenge is already open, so do pick up the phone, vote online or text GETRID and the number of the contestant on the screen in front of you."

"But what about the Golden Challenges, I hear you ask?" said Donald, even though no one had. "Well, I'll tell you. During the course of the competition, there will be three Golden Challenges. As tough as the Elimination Challenges are, they'll have nothing on these."

"The team that wins the most Golden Challenges will be our **End Games** champions," continued Ronald. "So as long as a team has one member left, they still have a shot at winning. Unlike Elimination Challenges, contenders for the Golden Challenges will be picked by the team themselves and… Er, yes?"

Everyone turned to look at Milo, who had his hand raised. "What happens if a team wins the first two Golden Challenges? They can't lose at that point, so do we just all go home?"

It was a fair point. Usually these shows ran for a set period of time. I couldn't think of any that could potentially finish early because of its own rules.

"Milo, I'm glad you asked that," said Donald.

"And the answer is yes. We get to go home early."

"But don't worry," said Ronald. "We still get paid the same."

"Um … we're not getting paid," said Lexi.

"You need to get a better agent, sweetie," said Bo, exchanging smirks with Bruiser.

"You need to throw out everything you ever thought you knew about reality TV," continued Donald. "This is going to be unlike anything anyone has seen before."

"I dunno," said Zizi, "I've done a LOT of reality shows."

"You've never done one like this," said Donald.

"Well, I did I'm a Cele—" said Zizi, before her microphone cut out, and Ronald and Donald began waving at her to stop.

"Whoa, whoa, whoa!" shouted Ronald. "We are certainly nothing like *that* show."

"Yes, any similarities or likenesses to preexisting reality shows are purely coincidental," said Donald.

"Right, let's get to the fun part," said Ronald. "Announcing the teams."

"The first person to be called," said Donald, "takes the tunnel on the left. The next person, the tunnel on the right. And so on. There you'll find supplies and further instructions. Ronald and I will see you all back here tomorrow afternoon for the first Elimination Challenge."

"So without further ado," said Donald. "The first name is: SAM!"

As I stood up and started walking toward the left tunnel, I glanced back at Milo and Lexi. There was a chance I wouldn't be on the same team as them. But worse still, there was a chance I wouldn't be on the same team as Nigel Cruul. As much as the idea of being near Cruul filled me with dread, it was crucial to the mission that I kept close to him at all times.

I walked out, blinking, into the daylight. I had only taken a few steps beyond the cave when I heard Ronald announce the first member of the other team.

"NIGEL!"

Great. That meant I'd have to hope that either Lexi or Milo ended up with him.

I followed a light dirt path through thick jungle until I came to a small clearing, where four wooden crates awaited. Attached to the top of the nearest one was an envelope with the following words written on the front: **ONLY TO BE OPENED IN FRONT OF ENTIRE TEAM**.

I could see a couple of cameras secured to the trees, pointing directly at me. I was pretty sure I was meant to ignore them, so that's exactly what I did. Or tried to anyway. I took a seat on one of the crates and waited for my next teammate.

"Just my luck to be stuck with the boy band weirdo," said Bo, pushing his way through the undergrowth.

I didn't bother to reply – I was too busy worrying about who our remaining members would be.

"Here's Zizi!" shouted Zizi as she burst through the foliage like a performer in a cabaret show. For some reason she seemed to find this hilarious. "Your faces," she kept saying, pointing at me and Bo.

"What's wrong with our faces?" asked Bo.

"I have no idea," I said.

"And here's Pierre!" she said as the pug popped out of the top of her T-shirt.

Zizi's appearance was a relief. With only one spot left it meant that at least Milo or Lexi would be able to monitor Cruul.

Just as it was occurring to me that I could be stuck on a team without either of them, Lexi walked into the clearing, looking a little annoyed.

"What's wrong?" I asked.

She shrugged. "Nothing. I was just hoping to be on the same team as Joe. I wanted to ask him more questions about his films."

I rolled my eyes. Bruiser would probably never know how lucky he had been to avoid Lexi's team.

"So … Milo's on the other side," she said. "With Cruul."

"Yeah," I said quietly. Suddenly it dawned on me what that actually meant. My best friend was by himself, on a team with the most dangerous man on the planet.

CHAPTER SEVEN

A|A
APOCALYPSE INTELLIGENCE AGENCY

"So now what are we meant to do?" asked Lexi.

"What's this?" said Bo, snatching the envelope off the crate. He opened it up and pulled out a card. The rest of us had to crowd around him to read it.

Welcome to Fin Del Mundo! It's time to get to know your new teammates. And what better way to do it than with some team-building exercises? In these crates, you'll find everything you need to set up your shelter. Enclosed is a map of the area allocated to you for building your new settlement. You'll have to move fast, though – you'll want to have your camp built before sunset!

And of course every team needs a name. Your other task will be to come up with a name that best represents the four of you.

Good luck!

"A name that represents us?" said Bo. "How about One Star and Three ... Not Stars?"

"Very clever," said Lexi.

Bo tossed the envelope away and grunted.

"What about ... Accelerate?" put in Zizi.

"What about it?" said Bo.

"As a name for the team," she said.

"It's dumb," said Bo.

"Oh? Is it?" said Zizi. "I quite like it. OK. What about Team Lush?"

"Or Team Dominus?" suggested Lexi.

"Dumb and Dumber," said Bo dismissively.

Zizi looked confused. "I'm not sure Dumb and Dumber is a very good team name, Bo."

"Yeah, not very inspirational," agreed Lexi.

"What? No, I meant... Oh, never mind," said Bo.

I picked up the envelope and removed another

piece of paper, which I unfolded to reveal a map of the island. As maps go, it was pretty basic. The only thing it showed was a path leading to a red X on an area of beachfront and a scale to tell us how far away it was. "Look, we should probably leave figuring out a name until later," I said. "We need to get our camp set up."

"Sam's right," said Lexi.

"And just how exactly are we supposed to move these crates?" asked Bo.

It was a good question. A quick shove of the nearest crate made it obvious that there was no way we were going to be able to carry one each.

"We'll have to do them together, one by one," I said.

Bo grabbed the map from my hands. "Is this where we're going?" he asked, pointing at the X. "That's got to be at least half an hour away. Lugging one of those things? Multiple times? No chance."

"Well, we don't have much of a choice, do we?" said Lexi.

Bo snorted. "You don't maybe, but I'm not breaking my back over this. I'm a professional athlete."

"You play video games," said Lexi.

"Exactly," said Bo. "What if I hurt my hands? That would be the end of my career. I've got my sponsors to think about. Nope, there's only one thing for it. You guys will have to carry them. Don't worry, though, I'll bring the map. Follow me." Bo snapped his fingers and marched off into the jungle, leaving the three of us in stunned silence.

"Remember back at the cave, when Joe said there weren't any laws on this island…" said Lexi, leaving the question hanging.

"It'd still be wrong to kill him," I said. "Come on, we'd better get started."

Several hours later me, Lexi and Zizi dragged the final box onto the beach. I was covered in sweat, and my hands were red raw. I just wanted to curl up and go to sleep. But with the sun already starting to go down, there was still loads to do. We had to set up camp and get ourselves something to eat. We also had to decide on a name.

Lexi and Zizi had spent most of the trips coming up with suggestions as Pierre yapped mercilessly at our heels the entire time. I didn't really care what we called ourselves, but they had taken it pretty seriously. Suggestions so far included:

- Survivalists
- Poseidon
- Champions
- Meerkats
- DANGER!!! (including exclamation marks)
- Orion
- Salsa
- Winners
- Ellipsis
- No Fear

There was a crowbar attached to one of the crates. I pulled it off and was about to start opening the lids when Bo snatched it from me.

"What are you doing?" I asked.

"I'm the greatest unboxer the world has ever seen," he declared. "If anyone's going to open these crates it's me."

"An unboxer?" I repeated.

Bo looked horrified. "Surely you're subscribed to my Un-Bo-Xing channel?" he said.

I shook my head. "Sorry."

"But you're what, fourteen?" he said. "You're my target demographic! What are you doing with your time if you're not watching me open things in an entertaining yet informative manner? Don't say watching TV. I don't think I could take it."

"We're really tired." I sighed. "Can you please just open the boxes?"

Bo tutted. "Fine, prepare to have your mind blown." He raised the crowbar and started prying the lids off the crates. All the while he gave a running commentary on the wood the crates were made out of (pine), his crowbar technique and how the boxes compared to previous boxes he had opened.

The first couple of crates contained two tents, some basic cooking equipment, a few meals' worth

of rations, our **End Games** uniforms and our
personal bags. But the contents of the final two
almost reduced the entire team to tears. Except Bo,
who thought it was hilarious.

One contained an attachable set of wheels that
looked useful for transporting crates from one
destination to another.

The other just contained rocks and a note that
said:

Hopefully you're reading this at the start of your
journey, not the end. An important life lesson – it's
important to think INSIDE the box!

"Why did they do that?" I said, completely
exasperated.

"Probably because it'd be funny for people at
home to watch you all wasting your time," sniggered
Bo.

Lexi looked like she was about to flip.

"Maybe we should just get the tents up,"
suggested Zizi.

"I'm starving," said Bo.

"Here you go," said Zizi, tossing him a loaf of bread.

Bo looked at it quizzically. "What am I meant to do with this?"

"Um … make a sandwich maybe?" snapped Lexi.

"Yes, fine, that'll do," he said, tossing it back to Zizi.

"Hey!" said Lexi, but Zizi just smiled.

"It's OK," she said. "I'm no good at tents. Why don't you three start on that, and Pierre and I will fix us all some sandwiches?"

"Sounds good," I said. "Thanks, Zizi."

Zizi fumbled around in the crate. "There's some ham here," she said.

Bo looked horrified. "I'm a vegetarian!"

"Oh … right … sorry," said Zizi. "Let's see then … cheese … lettuce … turkey… No, you won't want that."

"Turkey's fine," he said.

"But you just said you were a vegetarian," said Lexi.

Bo rolled his eyes. "I still eat white meat. That's OK."

"Pretty sure it isn't," I said.

"Um … let's see, who would know best?" said Bo. "You or me, a vegetarian since I was six and the presenter of VegVlog – the most watched vegetarian vlog of all time? I'm as strict as it gets. I only eat white meat, the occasional sausage and a bacon sandwich on Fridays."

"There's burgers here too," said Zizi.

"Chuck on a couple for me," said Bo, licking his lips.

"Right then," said Zizi. "I'd better build us a fire. Luckily I learned how on another reality show."

"One of those jungle shows?" asked Lexi.

Zizi shook her head. "No, it was that dance show, Strictly Come Prancing. I didn't do so well on that one…"

"Come on then," I said, turning to Bo. "Let's get the tents up."

"Yeah, you do that," he said. "And I'll go and record a diary entry."

"A what?" asked Lexi.

"You know," said Zizi. "It's where you sit in front of a camera in a room by yourself, telling the world your innermost thoughts."

"Exactly," said Bo. "And it's been almost twenty-four hours since I did that, so I might be some time."

"Where's the room?" I asked.

Bo pointed through the trees. "In that shed."

I had to squint to see it. "How do you know?" I asked.

"It's like a vlogger superpower I have," he said. "Wherever I am I can always sense where the nearest space to record a monologue is. Give me a shout when the burgers are ready."

Lexi and I set to work putting up the tents. Well, after whacking myself in the face with a tent pole and nearly knocking out my sister while trying to hammer in a peg, it's probably fairer to say that Lexi put the tents together, and I just held things in place. At least standing around gave me time to think about my own diary entry. It seemed the perfect chance to sneak a message to the **AIA**. Now I just had to figure out what that message would be.

CHAPTER EIGHT

In the end, it didn't matter. After returning briefly to wolf down his burger, Bo spent the rest of the evening hogging the diary shed. But even that didn't seem to be enough for him. Once he retired to the tent we were sharing for the night, he then proceeded to vlog in his sleep.

Just after midnight, and about half an hour into Bo sleep rambling about his favorite types of cheese, I decided to get some fresh air. As I stepped out of the tent, the cool sea breeze immediately made me feel much better.

There was a surprising amount of light from the moon, enough to make out most of our camp.

There were no camera people around now, but I could see a few cameras attached to various rocks and trees. I felt for the Time-Out device, still stuck firmly inside my hair. If I couldn't sleep I might as well start to explore the island.

I was just about to grab my shoes when I saw them. A hooded figure a bit of a way down the beach, looking out to sea. I quickly ducked behind the tent.

Who were they? A crew member? One of the other contestants? Maybe even Cruul himself? I had to find out. I put on my shoes, then fumbled with my hair for a few seconds, eventually finding and pressing the Time-Out button.

When I looked up they'd vanished. I ran toward where the figure had been standing, hoping to follow their footprints, but when I got there, there were none. The figure must have somehow found time to cover their tracks.

Keeping an eye out for any other mysterious figures, I reactivated the Time-Out device and started walking back toward camp. I was so busy looking around that I failed to see the rock in my path and tripped over, landing face-first in the sand.

Well, at least the cameras wouldn't have seen me do that.

I limped back to the tent and must have fallen asleep straightaway, as the next thing I knew it was light. The tent was hot and sticky in the morning sun, and my hair was plastered across my forehead. Bo's sleeping bag was empty, and from the sound of voices outside it looked like the others were all up already too.

I flung on some clothes and crawled out of the tent. Zizi, Pierre and Lexi were sitting around a fire, tucking into some sausages. They looked calm and refreshed, the opposite of how I felt.

"Morning," they said. Apart from Pierre, who barked.

"Sleep well?" asked Lexi.

I made a noncommittal grunting noise and looked around for Bo. Instead I spotted two of the camera crew having what looked like a heated discussion. "What's that about?" I asked.

"It's probably to do with what happened last night," said Zizi. "Apparently the cameras stopped working for a bit. They don't know why."

"Oh, right," I said. I could feel Lexi looking inquisitively at me. I'd have to try and find a way to tell her later. But first there was something else I had to do. "Where's Bo?"

"He's just headed over to the diary shed," said Zizi. "He wants to talk about his dream. You want me to cook you some sausages on the fire?"

"When I get back," I shouted, rushing into the jungle toward the diary shed.

Bo was just opening the shed door when I pushed past him and quickly locked it behind me.

"Hey!" he shouted, banging on the door.

I sat down on a stool in the center of the room. "Right, how does this work?" I said aloud, looking up at the fixed camera facing me.

"Hello, Sam, what would you like to talk about?" came a friendly sounding woman's voice through some speakers attached to the walls.

I had come to try and get a message to the **AIA,** but obviously I couldn't say that. I had to think of a way to sneak it into the conversation. What did people normally talk about on these shows? I tried to remember the times I had watched them with my parents. Usually it was just people bad-mouthing the other contestants behind their backs. That wasn't really me.

BANG! BANG!

"Open this door!" yelled Bo. "I want to tell them about my dream!"

On the other hand…

Half an hour later I realized I had spent the entire time complaining about Bo. I hadn't made any attempt to sneak a message in there.

In my desperation I found myself looking around for a coconut. Of course there wasn't one, and I could scarcely remember a single thing from Agent Speed's list anyway.

Then I had an idea.

"Zizi said she heard the cameras went off last night," I remarked.

A pause. "Yes," the voice said. "Briefly. Nothing to worry about."

I had to push further. Knowing one of the cameras would have filmed me reacting to the person in the hood, I had nothing to lose. "Just after midnight, I thought I saw someone," I said. "On the beach."

"Unlikely," she said, this time without any delay. "Probably just your mind playing tricks. Or if it was someone, it would have just been a crew member."

There was a defensiveness to her tone. I decided

to leave it there and opened the door.

"About time," said Bo. "You do realize there are other people on this team, don't you?"

As I walked back to join the others something dawned on me. These shows only lasted about an hour a day. What were the chances of the producers including a bit where I asked them about a technical fault? Not high, I imagined. Realistically, there was little chance the **AIA** were going to get my message about the figure on the beach. And even if they did, what exactly could they do about it?

The hooded figure might have been a crew member or a fellow contestant. After all, as far as I knew, Milo's team could be camped just down the beach from us. Or it might have been my mind playing tricks on me… If I wanted to find out, I was going to have to do it myself. But first there was an Elimination Challenge to get through.

CHAPTER NINE

"I just don't want to do one that has snakes," said
Zizi as we made our way back to the cave, later
that day. "I hate snakes. So does Pierre. Don't you,
sweetie?" Pierre gave a little growl in reply.

There were mixed feelings about the first
Elimination Challenge. For some reason Zizi
actually seemed excited about the prospect.
Because she had done so many of these shows
maybe elimination didn't really mean that much
to her. She'd be back on another one soon enough
anyway. And with his army of fans behind him,
Bo wasn't that bothered about it at all.

For me and Lexi there was too much at stake to

be excited. If either of us got sent home it was going to make it a lot harder to discover what Cruul was up to. I figured I was the likeliest to face the vote. Bo was one of the most obnoxious people I had ever met, but everyone knew he had a massive fan base. My fan base was basically my parents.

"Everything OK?" Lexi asked as we reached the chamber. I still hadn't found a moment to tell her what I'd seen.

"Let's find Milo," I said.

I immediately spotted him beside the stage, talking to Betty Black. I caught his eye and motioned for him to meet us at the back of the chamber next to a bunch of crates, away from the cameras.

"How's it going?" I asked.

"Fine," Milo said.

"Is that it?" I'd expected a bit more about his first day on *Team Cruul*.

Milo raised his eyebrows and gave his head a little scratch. Of course, the mics! I quickly ran a hand through my own hair and clicked the button on the

Time-Out. We looked back toward the stage, where the techs were now fussing over the cameras.

"So has Cruul done anything strange yet?" I asked.

Milo shook his head. "I've been watching him like a hawk, but actually he's been quite … well, nice."

I screwed up my face. "Nice?"

"I know!" said Milo. "I was as surprised as anyone."

"Well, it's an act, obviously," said Lexi. "For the cameras."

"Yeah. I'll keep my eyes peeled." Milo nodded. "I'm sure he'll show his real self sooner or later."

I told them about what I had seen during the night.

"Interesting," said Milo, rubbing his chin. "But I don't think it was Cruul. We're sharing a tent and I'm a pretty light sleeper. I think I would have heard him get up. Worth investigating, though."

"Tonight," said Lexi firmly. "We'll sneak out once everyone's asleep."

"Right," I agreed, before realizing we were overlooking one pretty important factor. "Hang on, what if one of us gets eliminated?"

A knowing smirk appeared on Lexi's face. "We won't."

"How do you know that?" I asked.

"Just something Bo told me while you were in the diary shed," she said. "Trust me, we're good."

"What about me?" asked Milo.

"Oh, come on," I said. "Unless you've gone out of your way to be offensive, the public aren't going to pick you. You're too popular."

Milo squirmed a little at this.

"I wonder what they have planned for these challenges anyway," I said, changing the subject.

"I hope that's not any indication," said Milo, pointing to one of the crates. The lid was half-open, and inside was an odd assortment of medical supplies, clocks and what looked like…

"Are those tranquilizer darts?" said Lexi.

"I think so. I wonder what…" Milo's voice trailed off as a cheer went up from the other end of the chamber. It looked like the cameras were back up and running.

"Can everyone take their seats," shouted Karen, looking stressed. "We go live in a few minutes. That's if nothing else goes wrong."

"That was a pretty mean trick they pulled with those boxes yesterday," said Milo as we headed to join the others.

"So you guys carried them all back too?" I said, feeling a rush of relief.

His face flushed a little. "Er…"

Before he could finish, Karen had grabbed him and led him to his seat. Not willing to incur her wrath, I sat down just as Ronald and Donald took to the stage.

A screen came down behind them, and a video started to play, showing highlights from the first day. It started with footage of our team lugging a crate across the island, then cut to Milo's team opening their boxes first. Next we saw Milo's team get both of their crates to their campsite in a single trip. They then spent the rest of the day setting up their tents, cooking a meal, playing in the water (not Milo obviously), talking, laughing and generally having a great time. Every so often it would cut back to our team, still lugging crates. All the while a clock at the bottom of the screen made it painfully clear just how long it took us. The whole thing ended with me accidentally dropping a crate on my foot.

While Milo's team couldn't move for laughing, our team squirmed in their seats through the whole thing. Apart from Bo, of course, who joined in the laughter. But that wasn't the worst of it. In among the footage there was a sequence that bothered me more than anything else. It only lasted a couple of seconds, a blink-and-you'd-miss-it thing, really, but it was there. Milo's team sitting around a campfire as

Cruul told a story. Though you couldn't hear what was being said, everyone was listening intently and laughing as Cruul delivered his punchline. Milo included. Milo then must have said something funny himself as Cruul burst into laughter, giving him a jovial slap on the back. I wasn't really sure what to make of it. Milo wasn't buying into the Nice Guy Nigel act, was he?

"All right, so a very good day for one team, a not so good day for the other," said Ronald once the video had ended.

"An important lesson to be learned there," said Donald.

"Definitely," agreed Ronald. "It's like my mom used to tell me: if you're ever asked to carry four huge crates across an island on a reality TV show, check what's inside them first."

"Your mom is so wise," said Donald.

"She is," agreed Ronald. "OK, so as well as moving boxes, we also gave the two teams the task of coming up with a name. Sam, what are you guys going to be called?"

"How about *The Transporters*?" suggested Donald, to more laughter from the other team.

"Um … no," I said. We had eventually settled on a team name, but now as the word formed in my mouth, I realized how awful it was. "Ellipsis."

There was a brief but awkward silence punctured by some tittering from Milo's team. "You mean like dot, dot, dot?" asked Ronald.

"We think it sounds a bit mystical," said Zizi.

"And we like the way it ends sentences on a note of suspense," said Bo. "That's like us – we plan on keeping people guessing."

I nodded. "Yep. What they said."

"That's terrible!" shouted Joe Bruiser.

"Oh yeah?" said Bo. "And what are you all called, then?"

"We're Team Accelerate," replied Bruiser.

"See, I told you we should have gone with that!" Zizi pouted.

"All right, all right," said Ronald. "So we have Team … Ellipsis – see what I did there? – and Team Accelerate. Excellent. Now we come to the exciting

95

bit. Revealing which of you have been chosen by the public to take part in the first **ELIMINATION CHALLENGE!**"

A gust of air swept through the cave, blowing out most of the candles. Spooky purple and red lights shot up from the stage floor, illuminating Ronald and Donald's faces.

"The public have voted," said Donald, putting on a somber voice. "The results have been verified. The first member of Team Ellipsis to face elimination is…"

"Bo!" shouted Ronald.

I turned to Lexi. She grinned back at me.

Suddenly Bo was lit up by a spotlight. To say he looked surprised was an understatement. "Well, obviously there must be some mistake," he said, laughing nervously. "I specifically instructed all my fans to vote for me. There are millions of them."

The chamber fell into an awkward silence. "Sorry," said Betty Black. "Did you say you've been *asking* people to vote for you?"

"Of course," said Bo. "Mobilizing the Bo Brigade

to vote to save me."

"It's a vote to nominate you, you mug!" Joe Bruiser cackled.

Bo's jaw hit the floor. "What? But I thought… Oh no! Wait, can we have a do-over on this one? There's been a huge misunderstanding."

"No second chances, I'm afraid," said Donald. "Now, our second contestant to face the Elimination Challenge, from Team Accelerate…"

"It's Nigel," said Ronald.

Another spotlight fell on Cruul. Unlike Bo, he took the news far better, smiling and nodding as if he'd been expecting it. Joe gave him a friendly slap on the back. But thankfully it appeared that the public wasn't buying Cruul's act, at least for now.

"So if we could have the two contestants join us onstage," said Ronald.

As Bo and Cruul made their way up, a table and two stools were brought on by a couple of crew members. A red-and-white checked cloth was then draped over the table and a small vase containing a single orange flower was placed in the center.

Ronald and Donald were now wearing berets with stuck-on oversized moustaches. "*Mes amis*, if you pleeze, take a seat," said Ronald, putting on a terrible French accent.

"*Oui*, be our guests," said Donald, whose effort was somehow even worse.

Bo and Cruul took their places, their eyes locked on each other.

"Now, ze first challenge," said Ronald, "it iz an eezy one. All you have to do iz be ze first to finish a special meelkshake and a nice boor-ger."

"A what?" asked Bo.

"A meelkshake," repeated Ronald. "And a boor-ger."

A crew member appeared with a silver tray and put down two large glasses in front of Bo and Cruul. Inside each was a pink-y, green-y, gray-y concoction with gross chunky bits throughout. Next to these he placed covered plates.

"Now zees meelkshake iz a leetle bit different to meelkshakes you've probably 'ad before, no?" said Donald.

Cruul looked repulsed but not nearly as much as Bo did.

"You're not expecting us to drink that?" he asked, even though it was pretty obvious that's exactly what was expected.

"*Oui*," said Ronald.

"Will you drop that ridiculous act and talk normally?" Bo snapped.

"Er … yeah, OK then," said Ronald.

Bo sniffed the top of his glass, before making a face like he was going to throw up. "What's in it?"

"I'm glad you asked," said Donald, removing a piece of paper from his pocket. "All natural ingredients, of course. Let's see… There are cockroaches, maggots, worms, crickets, dung beetles, actual dung, vomit fruit, fish eyes, fish guts, haggis, ants and kale."

"Not kale?" said Cruul, making a retching sound.

"I can't drink that," said Bo.

"Why not?" asked Ronald.

Bo looked around the chamber, scrambling for an answer.

"Because he's a vegetarian," sniggered Lexi.

"Yes, that's right, I am!" he shouted.

The video screen flickered into life again, playing footage of Bo tucking into a big greasy burger. The chamber erupted in laughter. I couldn't help feeling sorry for him, though.

"Fine," he whispered. He pointed at his plate. "And what's in there?"

"Oh, just another burger," said Ronald innocently. "The milkshake's to wash it down."

"That doesn't sound too bad, I guess," said Bo.

"Sorry, did I say burger?" said Ronald, slapping his forehead. "What I meant to say was **TARANTULA BURGER!**"

He pulled the covers off the plates to reveal two large buns. They looked like normal burgers, apart from the teeny-tiny difference of there being eight legs sticking out of the sides.

"Oh, come on!" Bo groaned. "Are they at least cooked?"

"Of course," assured Donald. "Cooked to perfection. Now the rules are exactly what you'd expect. The first to finish wins. Any more questions? Nope? We'll count down from three. You guys ready?"

Cruul nodded. With a grimace, Bo did the same.

"OK," said Ronald. "Three … two … one… Go!"

Cruul picked up his burger and took a huge bite. He gave a brief nod to indicate it wasn't that bad.

Bo wasn't quite as quick to get stuck in. Eventually he took a deep breath, picked up the burger and held it close to his mouth. For a moment it looked like that might have been as far as he'd go, but then he started to extend his tongue tentatively toward the edge of the burger. He was only half an inch away from touching it when it happened. The burger touched him.

101

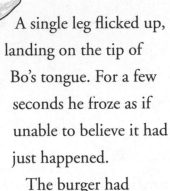

A single leg flicked up, landing on the tip of Bo's tongue. For a few seconds he froze as if unable to believe it had just happened.

The burger had moved – and in fact was still moving.

"AAAAAAARRRGGGHH!"

Bo flung the burger as far as he could. It sailed over our heads, landing with a thud. We watched as the tarantula wriggled free from the bun and dashed out of the cave to freedom.

Bo turned accusingly to Ronald and Donald.

"Don't look at us," said Ronald. "We didn't cook the thing."

"Neither did anyone else by the looks of things," Donald pointed out.

"Mine was cooked," said Cruul. "Medium rare, just the way I like it."

"I can still taste it on my tongue!" wailed Bo.

He grabbed the milkshake and took a huge gulp.

That was a mistake. Bo started projectile vomiting all over Ronald and Donald. Cruul, on the other hand, calmly drank the entire contents of his glass as though it were nothing more than a regular milkshake.

Cruul had won. Bo was gone.

CHAPTER TEN

AIA
APOCALYPSE INTELLIGENCE AGENCY

Voice: Hello, Sam. Could you talk us through the challenge?

Sam: Why? Don't you have it on tape?

Voice: Of course. But you know reality shows, half the time's taken up by people just recapping what everyone's already seen.

Sam: Right. Well, Bo lost. I hope he's all right. I suppose some of his color had come back when they were carrying him away on the stretcher...

Voice: And what did you make of Nigel's effort?

Sam: I guess I shouldn't be surprised he won. I know he's got the stomach for much worse. But the way he won... He didn't even flinch. He drank that thing like it was a normal milkshake. Are we sure it *wasn't* a normal milkshake?

Voice: What are you suggesting?

Sam: Like … there wasn't maybe a mix-up with the glasses or something?

Voice: [Serious] No.

I decided that there probably wasn't a lot to be gained from openly calling Nigel a cheat, so I left the diary room and returned to our camp.

"What's that?" I asked as I spotted my remaining teammates sitting on a log reading a sheet of paper.

"It's our punishment," said Lexi.

"For losing the Elimination Challenge," said Zizi, handing me the note. "They've cut our rations."

I think we can admit that was a bit of a flub,
And as punishment for losing, we've nicked all
   your grub.
So now if you scurvy bunch are wanting some food,
You'll need to go forage no matter your mood!

Not having to put up with Bo anymore had felt like a reward in itself so the news didn't come as a huge surprise. Still, the closest I'd come to sourcing my own food was going to the fish and chip shop for Gran.

Zizi, Pierre and Lexi went off into the jungle in search of fruit. I decided to go and fish.

Not having fishing equipment was a problem. I brought along a spare T-shirt, thinking I could use it as a makeshift net, and a pointy stick I found on the way down to the water to serve as a spear.

I spent about an hour throwing the stick into the sea. I didn't dare to venture out too far in case the shark came back. After all, the goal was for me to catch fish, not the other way around. There were plenty of fish to be caught, of every shape and size, but unfortunately there was a shortage of people equipped to catch them. The one time I did actually hit something the stick bumped off it and whacked me in the face.

After a while I switched to using the T-shirt. And then I saw it. A fish big enough to feed both teams, swimming lazily through the water. I positioned my "net" and held my breath as the monster fish continued blindly toward it.

"Gotcha!"

Gripping the "net" tightly in both hands, with all my strength I scooped it out of the water. But just as I raised it up, the fish sprang forward and head-butted me, sending me flying backward into the sea.

Coughing and spluttering, I rubbed the salt water from my eyes as the fish casually swam away.

Defeated, I decided to return to camp. With the sun beginning to set, my eyes drifted toward the huge mountain in the distance. It dominated the island, like a hulking bully having barged and shoved its way past the other kids to get to the best spot.

When I arrived back I couldn't believe my eyes. Lexi and Zizi were sitting in front of a massive pile of coconuts, bananas, mangoes, oranges, watermelons and tons of other mouthwatering fruits.

"Will that do?" asked Zizi, fetching me a towel.

There was enough there to last us weeks. "I think we'll be OK." I grinned.

When it was time for bed, Lexi and I entered our tents as normal and waited for Zizi to fall asleep before making our move. As I now had the tent to myself, I decided to leave the front unzipped as I waited for Lexi.

I gave a huge yawn. Hopefully she wouldn't be too long.

There was a rustling noise. I sat up and watched as the zip on the girls' tent started to pull up. It had only moved a couple of inches when Pierre started barking his tiny head off.

"Pierre!" said Zizi from inside the tent. "What is it, sweetums? Lexi, is everything OK?"

The zip was pulled back down, and I could

hear Lexi getting back into her sleeping bag. "Yep, all good," she said. "Thought I heard something. Nothing there, though."

"Oh, right," said Zizi. "Probably just some creature sniffing around. Don't worry. Pierre is an excellent guard dog." I heard her unzip the tent to let Pierre out. "Now keep watch. Good boy!"

Great. With Pierre on guard, Lexi wasn't getting out of the tent undetected. I was left with no option. I'd have to go by myself. I stood up quietly and took a step outside. Pierre started growling. I took another and the growling grew louder. With a heavy sigh, I decided to wait for a bit.

After half an hour, sure everyone had to be asleep by now – Pierre included – I started to edge out of the tent again. But I hadn't even gotten a quarter of the way when the growling started up. Undeterred, I left it an hour this time, but as soon as I made a move the growling commenced.

I had to abandon the plan, at least for the moment. What we needed was a Time-Out device for dogs…

CHAPTER ELEVEN

Voice: So who do you think is up for elimination today?

Sam: Oh me, definitely.

Voice: What makes you think that?

Sam: [Shrugs] Just a feeling, that's all.

That's the other thing I remember from these shows. No one ever comes out and says, "There's no chance of it being me, I'm just too popular." Well, Bo basically did, but anyone with any sense knows you have to be modest. Not that I didn't think there was a good chance of it being me.

There was a very good chance of it being me.

I shifted nervously in my seat as our hosts took to the stage.

"Today's contestant facing the Elimination Challenge for Team Ellipsis is … Lexi," announced Ronald.

Zizi and I turned to Lexi, but she had already sprung to her feet and bounded onto the stage.

"And she'll be up against…" said Donald. "Oh my, this is going to be interesting… It's Betty!"

There was a sharp intake of breath from both teams. I don't think anyone was expecting this. Least of all Betty, judging by the look on her face.

Adjusting her bouffant, Betty stood up. There was silence as she joined Lexi onstage.

"Oooh, youth versus experience," said Ronald, rubbing his hands together. "Everyone, follow us and we'll get started."

Ronald and Donald led us out onto the beach where two giant inflatable balls were waiting.

"These are called zorbs," said Donald. "Ronald, you like a good zorb, don't you, mate?"

"Oh yeah, I do love a good zorb," said Ronald. "Zorbing crazy, that's me. It's how I get around town."

"If you're not familiar with these bad boys," explained Donald, "the deal is you climb in, and then you start running. Like hamsters. Now you two have to channel your inner hamster in a head-to-head race."

Betty Black looked at the hosts like she was waiting for the punchline to a joke. "You're not expecting *me* to get in one of those?" she asked.

Ronald and Donald exchanged puzzled glances. "Um … yes, Betty," said Donald. "That's the challenge."

"But … but … my hair!" she said.

"Well, if you want to forfeit…" suggested Ronald.

"Fine!" She sighed. "So how do I get into that thing?"

"Good luck, Lexi!" I shouted as she and Betty were helped into their zorbs. I then made my way over to where Milo was standing.

"Hey," I said.

"Hey," he replied. "So ... good night?"

I shook my head. "Uneventful." I thought about pressing the Time-Out to ask for his advice on the Pierre situation but decided against it. I didn't want to risk anyone putting two and two together that the cameras kept cutting out every time we met up. Still, I was eager to know if he had made any progress at his end.

"How is life in Team Accelerate?" I asked. "Everyone getting along?"

Milo nodded. "Yeah, it's all right," he said. "I spent the day making a rudimentary sewage system."

"Sorry?" I asked.

"We've now got working toilets in our camp," he said excitedly. "They're very simple actually, built primarily using coconuts…"

"That's great, Milo," I said, conscious of how little time we had together, though admittedly a bit jealous. Our toilets were a lot less sophisticated – some holes we had dug in the jungle, a good distance from camp. It was too gross to think about. "So the whole team helped, did they? No one went off and did their own thing?" I tried to put emphasis on this last question.

"Well, Betty wasn't much help, if I'm being honest," said Milo. "She mostly just sits around complaining about all the people in television who've wronged her over the years, or is in her tent fussing with her hair. I probably shouldn't say this, but it wouldn't be the worst thing in the world if she got sent home."

"And … Cruul?" I asked.

"Complete opposite. He's going out of his way to be nice to everyone. He's like a totally different person."

I squinted at Milo. Was he trying to play the game here, by not criticizing Cruul on camera? Or was it something more sinister than that? It wouldn't be the first time I'd had to deal with people around me being brainwashed.

Milo must have read my thoughts. "I'm not brainwashed," he hissed, covering his mic.

So what was Cruul's game plan then? To come on the show and win people over? Hang on … was he actually trying to *win* this thing? It didn't seem like the most obvious way to bring back the Horsewomen. There had to be more to it than that.

Whatever the case, his act seemed to be working. He had saved Milo's life, come out of the first Elimination Challenge looking good and, from what Milo was telling me, was trying his hardest to make himself seem like a reformed character. Even I could imagine how well this was playing with the TV audience. Just as long as it didn't fool everyone.

I was about to remind Milo to be on his guard when Ronald and Donald called for silence. With Lexi and Betty inside their zorbs, the contest was about to begin.

"Hey, there's a little box taped inside here," shouted Lexi. "What's that for?"

"Oh, it's nothing to worry about," said Ronald, grinning. "So the course itself is pretty straightforward. It's a two-hundred-meter dash down the beach. The first to cross the finish line wins."

"Cam on, Betty!" yelled Bruiser. "You can beat that lil gel."

Lexi looked like she had just been punched in the gut. Bruiser was her idol – it had to sting hearing him insult her like that. But the hurt look on her face quickly turned to one of anger. Bruiser had just made her mad. And no one likes Lexi when she's mad.

"All right then, let's do this," said Donald. "Three … two … one…"

The zorbs trundled forward a little, taking a few seconds to build up speed. But it didn't take long before Lexi began to pull away from Betty.

After less than a minute, Betty seemed to give up, her zorb slowing down to the gentlest of rolls.

"Uh-oh," said Ronald and Donald, their faces filling with glee.

"You think we should've warned them about what would happen if their speed dropped?" asked Ronald.

"I think we probably should have, yeah," said Donald.

"What's gonna 'appen?" asked an intrigued Bruiser.

But Ronald and Donald didn't have to answer. Betty's zorb made a clicking noise. We could see her through the clear plastic, looking down at her feet.

"The little box is opening," shouted Betty. "Hey, what are those... **ARRGGGGGHHHHHH! SCORPIONS!**"

Tiny black creatures poured out of the box. As Betty scrambled to get away from them, her zorb shot forward.

"Wow, look at her go," said Zizi.

She wasn't kidding. Betty's zorb was rocketing down the beach. Lexi's lead rapidly began to shrink.

"Ha!" said Bruiser. "The old bird's gonna win."

With the finish line only meters away, Betty drew level with Lexi. Bruiser was right, Betty was about to steal this.

Suddenly Betty's zorb banked left, smashing into Lexi's and sending her flying off course.

"I think she did that on purpose," said Milo.

"Good on 'er!" Bruiser laughed. "Smart move, if you ask me."

Except it wasn't. Rather than continuing in the wrong direction, Lexi's zorb smacked into a palm tree. Like some giant game of pool, she ricocheted off it, hurtling back toward Betty. The two zorbs collided again, but this time it was Betty's that careened off to the right as Lexi's rolled over the finish line.

As Betty hurtled on down the beach, screaming the entire way, pretty much everyone rushed off after her. Everyone but me. I held back and then, when I was sure there were no cameras watching, I headed back to the cave.

CHAPTER
TWELVE

AIA

APOCALYPSE INTELLIGENCE AGENCY

Sam: How's Betty?

Voice: She's fine. Once she banged into that rock and knocked herself out the guys got her free pretty quickly. And considering she was going for about ten minutes the doctor thinks fifty-seven scorpion stings isn't that many. Relatively speaking.

Sam: But she's OK?

Voice: Sure, sure. Well, she should be... Anyway, let's talk about something else. Tomorrow is the first Golden Challenge. Have you come to a decision about who will represent Team Ellipsis?

Sam: No, not yet...

Voice: I should tell you that since they lost

today, Team Accelerate will have to announce their participant first.

Sam: So we'll be able to decide who matches up against their pick best?

Voice: Precisely.

As a reward for winning the challenge, we were treated to a hamper containing a few cans of cola, some dog food for Pierre and a huge fish. I'm pretty sure that was supposed to be a joke at my expense, but I didn't care – it was the tastiest fish I'd ever eaten. Zizi prepared it for us, using skills she had picked up on a show called Cooking and Karting.

"I think it was supposed to be like Top Gear meets Bake Off," Zizi said as we sat beside the fire after finishing our meal. "It wasn't that bad actually, but they had to cancel it after one of their features, 'Flan in a Van,' went horribly wrong."

"I was thinking about tomorrow," I said. "Maybe I should do the challenge?"

"Oh, I was hoping to have a try," said Zizi.

"I love doing challenges. Unless they've got snakes. Obviously."

"You said that we'd be able to announce our pick after Accelerate?" said Lexi.

"That's right," I said.

"If it's Bruiser, I'm doing it," she said in a tone that didn't invite a comeback. "If it's Cruul, then Sam can do it. If it's Milo, then Zizi, you're up. Fair?"

Zizi and I agreed. It made sense. I relished the thought of beating Cruul, but going up against my best friend wasn't as appealing.

We sat in silence for a while, staring up at the twinkling night sky as the fire crackled next to us. The sky was so clear – I had never seen anything like it back in London. There were so many stars it was like we were watching in HD. They seemed to fill the entire sky and the sea too. It was hard not to feel tiny and insignificant looking up at them.

I couldn't help but think about the Horsewomen and how they had tried to end all this. Not just the world but every star out there. All of it. And somehow, I, a tiny and insignificant speck in the universe, had stopped them. For now, anyway…

This was our third night on the island, and I was no closer to discovering what Cruul was up to. So far Milo hadn't come up with anything, and I was a little worried after our conversation earlier that he might be letting himself be taken in by Cruul's nice-guy act. I still thought that the hooded person I saw on the beach had something to do with him, and I was eager not to waste another night. Luckily I had a plan.

Before long, Pierre let out a yawn. "Oh dear," Zizi said, picking him up. "Someone's tired tonight. Think it's time we turned in. You coming, Lexi?"

"Yeah, in a bit," said Lexi, throwing me a quick glance.

"I'll see you both in the morning then," Zizi said. "Night."

"Night," we replied, trying not to look suspicious.

We waited about ten minutes.

"Well, good night, Sam," Lexi said as she walked toward her tent.

"Good night," I said, heading toward mine.

The moment we reached our tents, I ran a hand

through my hair and clicked the button on the Time-Out. We quickly removed our mics and tossed them inside.

And then we ran.

"I wasn't sure we'd get past Pierre," said Lexi.

"I had a feeling we would," I said, unable to resist giving her a little smirk.

Lexi gave me a curious look. "Sam… What did you do?"

"Well, when everyone was busy chasing Betty," I said, "I might have slipped back to the chamber and … borrowed one of those tranquilizer darts we saw. And then I might have broken it open and slipped a little bit into Pierre's food…"

"Sam!" said Lexi, looking shocked. "You drugged a pug?"

"It sounds bad when you say it like that," I said. "It wasn't much. Just enough to give him a good night's sleep. Oh, wait … this is it." We came to a stop at the part of the beach where I had seen the hooded figure.

"So what's the fastest way to get out of sight from here?" Lexi said, looking around.

We saw it at the same time. A small ridge in the sand, leading to the jungle. It wasn't something you'd be able to see from our camp, especially in the dark, so if someone had flung themselves to the ground they could have crawled away without being seen.

"Come on," said Lexi, walking toward the trees.

It was only as we got closer that I realized what a completely ridiculous idea it was to head into a jungle in the dead of night.

I heard a click, and a beam of light shot from Lexi's hand.

"Where did you get a flashlight from?" I asked.

"Bill, one of the camera guys," she said. "He lent it to me in case I needed to go to the bathroom in the night."

"Nice one," I said.

However, the farther into the jungle we walked, the less convinced I was that having the flashlight was a good thing. Every which way we turned we found ourselves staring into a new set of eyes of a creature that quickly vanished in fright. But the real fear was the thought of coming across something

that didn't run away.

It was slow going, having to watch our step at every turn. And it didn't really help that we had no idea where we were heading or even what we were expecting to find, beyond hoping that we'd run into someone dressed in robes. And then what? *Excuse me, robed person? Would you mind explaining yourself?*

"We should go back," I said eventually.

"Shh," Lexi said, grabbing my arm.

I heard it too. The sound of rustling in the trees up ahead. Lexi switched off the flashlight, and we crouched down behind a large log. Moments later another light lit up the space we had been standing in, only this one was of the fire-on-the-end-of-a-piece-of-wood variety.

Then we heard footsteps.

We held our breath as they approached. Two hooded figures stepped into the exact spot we had been standing in just moments before.

They stopped. Their torches spun back and forth, coming within inches of where we were hiding. They must have stood there for just a second or two, but it felt like minutes.

Without saying a word, the pair disappeared into the jungle the way we had come.

"Are they looking for us?" whispered Lexi.

"I don't know," I said. "But we should get out of here."

"What?" said Lexi. "We need to follow them."

She was right. This was our only lead. We couldn't let it slip through our hands. "Come on, then," I said.

We took a step, and then we found ourselves falling.

CHAPTER THIRTEEN

AIA
APOCALYPSE INTELLIGENCE AGENCY

"Lexi, you OK?" I asked, slowly sitting up.

"Think so," she groaned. "You?"

"I'll live," I said, rubbing my lower back. I looked up to see a moonlit outline of the hole we had stepped into. It had to have been at least a ten-foot drop.

I jumped as I heard a click, but it was just Lexi switching on her flashlight, which had also thankfully survived the fall.

"Whoa!" she said.

"Whoa!" I agreed.

We were inside a cave. Even without a flashlight I had been able to guess that much. It was far smaller than the one used for the show, but it was the walls that had us in awe.

They were covered in paintings, the kind done tens of thousands of years ago. But instead of mammoths and men with spears, the images were a lot more familiar. They depicted what must have been hundreds of hooded figures, like the ones we had just seen. As Lexi moved the flashlight beam along the wall, it became clear that rather than being lots of individual drawings, the figures were all part of the same scene. They were moving toward something … following some kind of trail … of smoke…

I let out a gasp. The flashlight tumbled from Lexi's hand. She picked it up, her hand trembling as she shone it back on the wall.

The image was crude, but there was no mistaking what it was. There, flying around a volcano, were four horses, ridden by four identical girls.

"It's them," I said, my voice barely a whisper.

"What does it mean?" asked Lexi.

"I don't know," I said. "But if there was ever any doubt that the Horsewomen and this island are connected, I think this pretty much ends that."

"Those people in the hoods," said Lexi, "are they worshipping them?"

"Looks like it," I said. "Maybe they're the original Apocalytes."

"Those two we saw out there," said Lexi, pointing up at the hole. "You think that's who they are?"

"This painting is probably thousands of years old," I said.

"So?" she replied. "This island just appears from nowhere. Maybe it time traveled here or came from another dimension. Or maybe it was like that Atlantis place, and it was under the ocean the whole time. And maybe those people have been hibernating. And now they're awake and ready to bring back the Horsewomen."

I didn't reply. At this point, anything seemed possible.

"We should go," I said. "What if someone finds us here? There must be a way out."

Lexi shone the flashlight around, looking for an exit. Just when it seemed we might be doomed to spend the rest of our days trapped inside a cave, Lexi spotted a narrow gap in one of the walls, a few feet above a small rockfall.

"It's worth a try," she said, and started to climb, sending a shower of stones bouncing down behind her.

I watched from a safe distance away as she squeezed her way through the gap, then followed.

The rocks were wobblier than I'd expected, and the gap was only just big enough for me to fit through. I breathed a sigh of relief as I finally emerged into the jungle near a small stream.

Lexi was crouched beside it. She reached a hand into the water and splashed some over her face. "That's better!"

I quickly did the same. Then we carefully made our way back to the hole we had fallen through, before retracing our steps back to camp.

As we walked in silence, one thing became clear – I had to get a message to the **AIA**.

CHAPTER FOURTEEN

APOCALYPSE INTELLIGENCE AGENCY

Voice: Hello, Sam. All set for the Golden Challenge?

Sam: I guess. I didn't sleep very well.

Voice: Oh?

Sam: Yeah, I thought I heard STRANGE voices during the night. I envy PEOPLE who can sleep through anything. I'm always LOOKING FOR SOMETHING to help me sleep better. But I've YET TO FIND IT.

Voice: [Pause] Are you all right? Your voice keeps going up at weird moments.

Sam: It's a bit HOARSE. WHOA, MAN it is.

Voice: Would you like to see the doctor, Sam?

Sam: Er … no. I'm OK.

Voice: Well, the sounds you heard were probably just some of the crew trying to fix the cameras in your camp. We had another outage last night. Two in fact...

Obviously I'd had to activate the Time-Out a second time when we got back. I acted surprised and left the diary shed as quickly as I could. Hopefully they'd air the footage. Even if the **AIA** got my message, there probably wasn't much for them to act on. But at least I'd tried.

I had managed to get some sleep in the end, but I was still pretty shattered, so I was grateful for the fact that most of the day was spent waiting around for the challenge. While Zizi took a slightly drowsy Pierre for a walk, and Lexi worked through some solo judo drills, I considered my next move. The sight of me sitting around staring into space probably didn't make for exciting TV, but it did help me get some of my thoughts in order. I had a lot of questions, but the biggest ones were:

1. What were those hooded figures doing wandering around the jungle last night?

2. How were they connected to Cruul?

I was no closer to an answer by the time the Golden Challenge came around. We had been warned that these would be a level above what we had seen so far, but nothing could have prepared us for this.

We were led deep into the jungle until finally we came to a stop on the edge of a vast river. In the middle was a rocky island, no more than a few feet wide. On the bank sat two wooden barrels with paddles. Ronald and Donald hadn't gotten around to explaining the contest yet, but I think we had pretty much figured it out.

A sudden movement beneath the surface of the cloudy water caused everyone to flinch. There was something in there. Something big. It quickly became clear it wasn't alone.

"Are you 'avin' a giraffe?" said Bruiser, who was – as Lexi had hoped – representing Team Accelerate.

"No giraffes – or laughs – here, Joe," said Ronald. "Just a lot of alligators."

"Correction," said Donald. "*Hungry* alligators."

"So we've got to reach that island in those barrels?" asked Lexi.

"Not just reach it," said Ronald. "You'll have to return from it too. Somewhere on that island is a special Golden Artifact. The winner will be whoever brings it back."

"What if one of us gets eaten?" cried Joe, looking over at Lexi for support.

"Then I'll dedicate my win to you," said Lexi.

"Yeah, right," scoffed Bruiser. "Like I'm losing to some pigtailed princess."

"Like I'm losing to some balding Z-list wannabe tough guy," snapped Lexi.

"I'm not balding!" shouted Bruiser.

"OK, OK, you two!" Donald laughed. "You're agitating the crocs."

"Alligators," corrected Ronald.

"What's the difference?" said Donald.

"I dunno." Ronald shrugged. "All I know is every time we say the wrong one we get thousands of people on the internet correcting us."

"Good point. Alligators it is. Right, contestants, if you can make your way to your barrels."

Lexi gave me a thumbs-up as she walked down to the riverbank. "Good luck," I mouthed.

"They'll be all right," said Milo, joining me.

"How can you be sure?" I said.

"Well, it's a TV show," he said. "They've probably fed the alligators beforehand. And look, there's a guy over there with a rifle. Must be what those tranquilizer darts were for. The producers are hardly going to put them in a situation where they can be eaten in front of millions of people watching at home."

I hoped he was right.

"On the other hand," said Zizi, catching the end of our conversation. "You'd be amazed how often things go wrong on these shows. They just don't show the footage. Especially if someone dies."

We both looked at her. "People … sometimes die?" I asked.

"Oh yeah, happens all the time," she said. "Most of the really dangerous shows I go on make you film a bit before it starts where you pretend that you're leaving for … I dunno, family reasons or something. That way if you snuff it, they just show the footage and cover it up. That's what happened to Danny Donovon on *So You Want to Be a Zookeeper?*"

"Who?" asked Milo.

"Exactly," said Zizi, tapping her nose. "Anyway, that was a freak accident. I mean, what are the odds of a tiger finding its way into someone's trailer? Especially after I locked it in its enclosure, like, half an hour earlier? At least I think I did…"

Milo and I just stared at her.

"I'm sure Lexi will be fine, though…" she said, smiling reassuringly.

Lexi and Bruiser, looking much paler than I remembered him being, had climbed into their barrels. Ronald and Donald stood behind them.

"OK," said Ronald. "Everyone ready?"

The hosts shoved the barrels into the water.

Hearing the splash, a few of the alligators glanced over at the barrels. Luckily they then seemed to decide they weren't that interested. As Lexi and Joe began warily paddling across the river, I started to relax a little. It looked like Milo was right about the alligators' lack of appetite. Better still, Lexi was starting to take the lead over Bruiser. Everything was going to be all right.

Now why did I have to go and think that?

Everything wasn't all right. Lexi's barrel was sinking.

CHAPTER FIFTEEN

"Er ... guys, bit of a problem here!" shouted Lexi.

"Why are you sinking?" I yelled as we all rushed down to the riverbank.

"I don't know," she said, "but it might have something to do with this **MASSIVE HOLE!**"

With her barrel rapidly filling with water, the river's nonhuman residents appeared to be taking more of an interest in the challenge. Several of the alligators were already slowly swimming toward Lexi, who was halfway between the bank and the island, and about to go under at any moment.

"Oh dear, oh dear," said Bruiser, grinning as he passed her. "Looks like *I'll* be the one dedicating

their win. I'll mention it when I give your eulogy.
At your funeral. 'Cause you'll be dead."

"Yeah, I got it, thanks. And we'll see about that,"
said Lexi as the barrel finally capsized, leaving her
clutching her paddle in the middle of the river.
Keeping calm, she held on to the wood with one hand
and started swimming with the other. But instead of
heading back, Lexi continued toward the island.

"What's she doing?" asked Milo.

"Trying to win." I sighed.

More and more of the alligators were eyeing Lexi
now, and some were already too close for comfort.
She started using her paddle to try and keep them
at a distance, but this didn't seem like a great long-
term plan to me.

"Come on, man, hurry up!" shouted Nigel Cruul, striding over to the guy with the rifle, who was nervously trying to load a tranquilizer dart into it. "Why haven't you already got the thing loaded?"

"I… I … d-d-didn't really expect to have to u-u-use it," stammered the guy, his hand shaking as he finally got the cartridge in. He raised the gun, pointed it at the alligator nearest Lexi and pulled the trigger. Nothing happened.

"M-m-must be j-j-jammed," he said. He turned the rifle around to inspect it.

The dart hit him in the side of the neck. There was a brief moment where the guy realized what had happened before he tumbled to the ground.

There was a collective groan.

"Oh, for goodness' sake," said Cruul, snatching up the rifle and the box of cartridges lying on the ground.

"What are you doing?" I said, stepping in front of him.

"What does it look like I'm doing?" he replied as he loaded the rifle.

"It looks like you're about to fire tranquilizer darts near my sister," I said.

"Yes," said Cruul. "Near your sister. Not *at* her. Now get out of the way, you twit, while I save her life."

With that, Cruul shoved me aside. He took aim and fired at the first alligator, who had just snapped off a piece of Lexi's paddle in its jaws. As the animal was about to move in for its real prize, the sedative must have kicked in, and it disappeared beneath the water. With ruthless efficiency, Cruul worked his way through the rest, firing and reloading until all but one of the alligators was asleep.

Of course, it was the "but one" part that was the problem.

"There are no more cartridges," said Cruul, tipping over the empty box.

My stomach lurched. I had taken one of the darts to get Pierre out of the way, and now Lexi was about to pay the price.

"She's on her own now," said Cruul.

We looked on in horror as the last alligator

charged at her. Lexi had discarded what was left of her paddle and was now swimming as fast as she could toward the island. Bruiser, meanwhile, was busy trying to climb out of his barrel. The process seemed to be taking longer than you'd expect, as he kept stopping to check there were no other alligators nearby.

As fast as Lexi was going, the alligator was much faster. There was no way she would outswim it. I couldn't just stand by and watch. I flung off my shoes and was about to dive in when several arms grabbed me.

"Sam," said Milo. "It won't do any good."

"We can't just let that thing eat her!" I said.

"I know, but…" Milo's voice trailed off. He had that look on his face he gets when he's had an idea.

"What is it?" I asked.

"Lexi!" yelled Milo. "Hair bands! Use your hair bands."

"Her hair bands?" I said, grabbing Milo and shaking him. "That's your plan?"

"Trust me," he said.

Lexi seemed to have realized that she couldn't outpace the alligator and had come to a stop. She was now treading water and facing the beast down. It was only a few feet away. I wasn't sure she had even heard Milo until she started fumbling with her braids, trying to take out one of her hair bands. Just as she finally succeeded, the alligator dived toward her, and she vanished beneath the water.

CHAPTER SIXTEEN

The entire world went silent after that.

I stared at the murky water where Lexi had been only seconds before, the ripples still visible, barely moving as time itself seemed to grind to a halt.

"Lexi!" I screamed, trying to escape Milo's grip.

"There's no way she could have—" began Cruul.

"Be quiet!" I shouted, not letting him finish the sentence. "Milo, tell him he's wrong."

Milo's mouth opened and closed, but nothing came out.

I looked back at the river. How much time had passed? Ten seconds? Twenty? How long could she hold her breath for? Longer than she could fight off an alligator? Hope faded with every second.

It was all but gone when Lexi exploded out of the water, gasping for air. My first reaction was to scream with joy, until I remembered that the alligator was still down there too.

A split second later the alligator burst to the surface. But as it thrashed around in the water it was clear its jaws were clamped tight. From where I stood I could just about make out the red hair band wrapped around its snout.

"See, I told you!" said a giddy Milo.

"But how?" I asked.

"It's simple really," he said. "Alligators and crocodiles have enormous power in their jaws, but most of it's in their bite. Their muscles are seriously bad at opening their jaws. You can stop them with a—"

"Hair band!" I finished. "Milo, you're a genius!"

"I just saw it on a documentary," he said. "Lexi still had to get it on the thing."

"I guess you could say that its bite is worse than its bark," said Ronald.

"Yes, you could say that, if you happened to be a complete idiot," said Cruul.

By now Lexi had made it to the island. Like the rest of us, Joe Bruiser had barely moved, watching the drama unfold with horrified fascination. Lexi marched toward the center of the island, shoving Bruiser out of the way as she passed. She knelt down and picked something off the ground. I caught a brief flash of gold as she walked back to Bruiser's barrel and tossed the object inside. Then she hopped in after it.

A bewildered Bruiser seemed to snap out of his daze. "Hey, that's mine!" he shouted as Lexi started paddling back toward us.

"Not anymore," said Lexi.

"Well, what am I meant to do?" he cried.

"Swim," she said.

By the time a reluctant Bruiser had plunged into

the water, Lexi had already made it back to the bank.

Milo and I helped her out of the barrel.

"Lexi," I whispered. "I thought…"

But Lexi wasn't in the mood for emotional displays of affection. She was more in the mood for emotional displays of rage.

"Congratulations to Lexi, the winner of—" began Donald, before Lexi grabbed hold of his shirt.

"Why was there a hole in my barrel?" she said. "Was me nearly dying supposed to be funny?"

"No!" said Donald. "We don't know how that could have happened. They should have been checked beforehand."

"Are you saying someone put that hole in there?" demanded Lexi.

"Lexi, I understand you're upset—" said Ronald.

"**YOU THINK?**" shouted Lexi.

"But I don't think any good can come from suggesting things like that," Ronald continued. "Whoever was supposed to check the barrels clearly

148

didn't do their job properly. Obviously they missed it, and that's completely unacceptable."

"Unacceptable?" she said. "I nearly got *eaten*!"

"Rest assured we'll have this investigated thoroughly," he said. "But ... you are OK. And not just OK, you only went and won! You retrieved the Golden Artifact which was a... Actually, what was it?"

"Dunno," said Lexi, who hadn't bothered to remove it from the barrel. "Some silly plate."

"Brilliant," said Ronald. "We're now going to bring the artifact back to the cave where we can officially record Team Ellipsis as the first winner of a Golden Challenge. And there might just be some special rewards in store for your team tonight."

"If it's not too much trouble," added Donald, "is there any chance you can let me go?"

Lexi released his shirt. "Thank you," he said. "And can I mention one thing? Can we all appreciate that an eleven-year-old girl ... just beat a crocodile in a fight!"

149

"Alligator," corrected Ronald.

"Oh, whatever," he said. "How about a round of applause for Lexi?"

As a cheer went up, Lexi's anger seemed to slip away, and the beginnings of a grin started to break through. Not everyone was cheering, though. A saturated Joe Bruiser emerging from the river for one, but that was understandable. It was the expression on Nigel Cruul's face that gave me most concern. He looked absolutely livid. This wasn't the look of someone annoyed that his team had lost a challenge. It was way more intense and angry than that. Then Cruul seemed to notice me staring at him because his face suddenly shifted, and he was applauding along with everyone else.

For just a few seconds Cruul's mask had slipped. The question was: why?

CHAPTER
SEVENTEEN

APOCALYPSE INTELLIGENCE AGENCY

AIA

"It doesn't make any sense," said Lexi. "Why would Cruul be mad about me not dying? He saved my life."

"No, he *almost* saved your life," I corrected her. "Isn't it convenient that he ran out of darts with one alligator left?"

"Wasn't very convenient for me," said Lexi.

"You know what I mean."

"Well, there would have been enough darts if you hadn't—" said Lexi.

"I know, I know," I said.

When we got back to camp I decided to use the Time-Out button again to speak to Lexi in private.

We still had to keep our voices down though, as Bill tried desperately to get things working again while Karen hovered impatiently around him.

"I'm sick to the back teeth of this," he grumbled, pressing several buttons on his camera before whacking it with a screwdriver. "It's me that gets it in the neck."

"You that gets it in the neck?" repeated Karen. "You want to try having a dozen people yelling in your earpiece all day."

"Yeah, well, this is what happens when you buy cheap equipment," muttered Bill.

While Bill grumbled away and continued to hit things, Zizi hovered over the campfire, cooking everyone a victory meal. One of our rewards for winning was an entire chicken. Lexi and I had both offered to cook, but Zizi had insisted. Which was handy because neither of us knew the first thing about cooking a chicken.

"I think that might be it…" said Bill.

I quickly ran a hand through my hair and pressed the Time-Out button again. Bill let out a series of words, which ironically you wouldn't want aired on TV.

"I'm just struggling to see Cruul's angle in all this," said Lexi. "Let's look at the facts. First he saves Milo, then he saves me… OK … almost saves me. But think about it. If he's still in league with the Horsewomen, why try to save the lives of two of the people who helped bring the Horsewomen down?"

I decided to turn the argument back on her. "So it's not at all suspicious that two of the people who helped bring the Horsewomen down have both *needed* their lives saving?"

"Not really," she said. "I mean it's obviously a dangerous show. We're on an island with no health and safety laws. This is probably a reality TV producer's dream. And I can't see how he'd have been able to make sure Milo landed in the sea."

"Are you really telling me you don't think Cruul's in on this?" I asked, unable to hide my disbelief. "That it's just a coincidence that the Horsewomen's right-hand man comes on a reality TV show on the island home to their weird hooded followers?"

"No," she said. "That's not what I'm saying. Of course Cruul's up to something. I just can't see what it is. Nothing he's doing makes any sense. Not that he's actually doing much. Milo still hasn't seen him acting out of the ordinary, has he?"

"Not that he's mentioned, anyway," I said.

Lexi gave me a funny look. "What do you mean by that?"

"I don't know." I shrugged. "I'm just starting to wonder if Milo is giving this his full attention. While he's spending his days building stuff, what's Cruul up to? Are you seriously saying that Cruul hasn't done a single thing worth reporting to us since he got here? I bet you anything he was under one of those hoods."

"But Milo would have heard him leaving camp," said Lexi. "He's a light sleeper, remember?"

"Maybe," I said. "Or maybe he's gotten too close to Cruul. Maybe he's fallen for the Nice Guy Nigel act, and he's not noticing things he should anymore?"

Lexi frowned and was about to reply when she

was interrupted by the sound of a celebrating Bill.

"Ha! We're back in business," he cried. "Must have been the last thump that did it. If you ask me, it's this island. Its magnetic fields must be out of whack or something."

"Finally," groaned Karen.

I decided against pushing the Time-Out button again. Lexi looked at me, her face full of frustration. Clearly she wanted to defend Milo. "You're wrong," was all she could say. I only hoped she was right.

"Dinner's almost ready!" Zizi shouted over.

"There's one other treat before that," said Karen, handing my sister her tablet. "This is for Lexi. Though I guess it'll be of interest to you too, Sam."

"What are we supposed to do with this?" she asked. But before Karen could answer, the tablet started to ring. Lexi swiped the screen and two familiar faces appeared.

"MOM! DAD!" she shouted.

CHAPTER EIGHTEEN

APOCALYPSE INTELLIGENCE AGENCY

"Lexi!" they shouted back. "Sam!"

I couldn't believe it. It felt like forever since I'd last seen my parents. Seeing their faces again made me realize how much I'd missed them.

"Lexi, are you all right?" asked Dad. "We couldn't believe it when we saw what happened."

"I'm fine," said Lexi. "Just a few scratches, nothing serious."

"Nothing serious?" repeated Mom. "You were almost eaten by an alligator."

"Honestly, I'm OK," said Lexi.

"It'd take more than that to stop our little girl," said Dad.

"Not that much more…" admitted Lexi.

"I've just been on the phone with the production company," said Mom. "Giving them a piece of my mind. That's why they agreed to let us talk to you. Don't believe any of their garbage about rewarding you. That was all just to shut me up."

"Well, we're glad to see you anyway," said Lexi.

"And, Sam, how are you getting on?" asked Dad.

"I've not had anything try to eat me," I said. "So better than some, I guess."

"You're coming across so well," said Mom.

"I am?" I said.

"He is?" said Lexi.

"Of course," said Mom. "You're all anyone's talking about."

"Why?" Lexi and I asked together.

"Yeah, why?" asked Zizi, looking up from the fire.

"All those bits where you fall on your face…" said Mom. "And watching you put up that tent. You're comedy gold."

"Oh and there's the fishing!" Dad laughed.

I had to think for a moment what he was talking about. "Fishing? From the other day?" I said.

My parents nodded. "Well, and yesterday too," said Mom.

Yesterday? "But I didn't—" I began.

"It's so funny, watching you struggle to catch something every day," interrupted Dad. "That bit where the stick whacks you in the face. It still cracks me up thinking about it. You've become a memo!"

"A memo?" I said. "What are you talking about?"

"Not a memo." Mom sighed. "A meme. You've become a meme. There's clips of you all over the internet."

"That's right," said Dad proudly. "You've gone infected!"

"Viral, dear," corrected Mom. "Anyway, you're doing a great job. Keep it up."

It suddenly occurred to me then that the **AIA** might be using my parents to communicate. "Um … any other messages?" I asked. "Of support, I mean."

"No, not really," said Mom. "Actually, there was something else we had to say to Lexi."

My parents put on their stern faces.

"Your judo instructor Mr. Yoshida called," said Mom. "He told us you missed a few practices."

Lexi stared at them blankly. "I've been on a desert island, Mom."

"Very funny," said Mom. "He meant before you left. He says you skipped every class last week. Is that true?"

Lexi looked away and made a noncommittal grunting sound.

"What's going on?" asked Dad.

"Nothing," she said. "I just wasn't feeling well."

"Are you sure that's all it is?" said Mom.

"Yes!" snapped Lexi.

Mom and Dad's heads rotated to the right as we heard someone mumbling something at their end. "Oh, apparently that's our time up," said Dad. "I guess we'll speak to you again soon."

"Yeah, bye then," muttered Lexi.

"Oh, Sam, before we go, has Milo spoken to you yet?" asked Mom.

"About what?" I asked.

Mom didn't reply. "Nothing, never mind. Bye, you two. Look after each other."

They hung up, and Zizi appeared next to us with two plates of the most amazing-smelling roast chicken ever.

"This is for you," she said, handing Lexi hers. "And this is for the Chosen One."

I almost dropped the plate she had just given me. "What did you call me?"

Zizi grinned as she fetched her own dinner. "Oh, come on, you must have figured it out."

I looked at Lexi, but I could tell she had no idea

either. When you've been referenced in an ancient prophecy as the only person who can stop the Four Horsewomen of the Apocalypse, the term "Chosen One" takes on a whole new meaning.

"You were trying to catch a fish for about an hour," explained Zizi. "But from what your parents said it sounds like the producers have been playing around with the footage, cutting it up so they could use it over different days."

"They'd really do that?" asked Lexi.

"Of course," said Zizi. "When I was on Carpool Orchestra they actually edited the footage so that I ended up having an argument with someone who wasn't even in the car at the same time as me."

"But why?" I said, before looking up at the cameras. They probably didn't want us talking about stuff like this.

Zizi laughed. "Oh, don't worry, they won't use any of *this* footage," she said. "You want to know why they'd go to the trouble? These shows are about telling stories. And someone's obviously decided you're the main character."

"Are you saying they want me to win?" I asked.

Zizi shrugged. "Now that's hard to say," she said, feeding Pierre a bit of chicken. "Maybe. But they definitely wanted you to get this far."

I realized Dad hadn't mentioned the bit where I got head-butted by a fish. I wondered if that was still to come. Were the producers really trying to keep me on the island? And, if so, why?

I wondered if Zizi was exaggerating, but then, the following day, her name was announced for the Elimination Challenge.

"I don't get it," I said, turning to Zizi.

"Me neither," said Lexi. "I thought people loved you."

Zizi smiled. "Yeah, but I'm up against the Alligator Queen and the Chosen One. I didn't stand a chance. Now can you guys keep an eye on Pierre while I do this thing? I just hope it's not snakes…"

The nominee for Team Accelerate was less of a shock. Bruiser could hardly have expected to avoid the vote after his performance in the Golden Challenge.

Ronald and Donald led them through the jungle to a watering hole about the size of a large wading pool. There were no alligators this time, but Zizi's

worst fears were realized. The pool was full of snakes
of all different colors and sizes. I glanced over at
Zizi, expecting to see a look of horror. But to my
surprise there was a faint grin on her face. She threw
me a wink.

I couldn't help but laugh. Zizi had been playing
the producers all along. Everyone seemed to think
she was dim, but there was a lot more to her than
people knew.

Someone did look genuinely scared, though. Joe
Bruiser.

"All right, everyone!" shouted Karen. "We're
taking a commercial break. We'll be back in a couple
of minutes."

"I wonder if they'll remove the snakes after the
challenge?" said Milo. "I could probably convert
this into a jacuzzi. Our camp's just along that path
there."

I turned my head to where he was pointing,
through a couple of bushes. Was Milo trying to tell
me something? I thought about pressing the Time-
Out button, but I wasn't sure I'd be able to get away

with it with so many people around.

"Of course the trick's going to be getting the bubbles in. I wonder if—"

"How's it going, anyway?" I asked, cutting him off.

"Yeah, OK," he said. "I just finished installing showers this morning. They're pretty basic, but they do the job."

I gave myself a sniff. *Eurgh.* Even Pierre at my heels smelled better. Showers sounded like heaven.

"Yeah, that's great," I said. "Any *other* news?"

"Nope," he said. "Nothing else exciting. Nothing at all."

All this time and still nothing? Or was Milo being coy because the cameras were on? Cruul couldn't really have done nothing all week. I made up my mind – I had to get into their camp. But how?

If I could somehow slip away while everyone was focused on the challenge then I'd have the camp to myself. But the only way to get past the cameras was to use the Time-Out device. And if I did that while the challenge was going out live they'd probably have to abandon it.

"Right, everyone, we're coming back!" shouted Karen.

"Welcome to today's Elimination Challenge," said Ronald to camera. "It's Zizi versus Joe. And as you've probably gathered, behind us is a pool full of snakes."

"Oooh, I hate snakes!" said Donald.

"I suspect you're not alone," said Ronald, smirking at Zizi, who put on a fake look of concern.

"You'll notice that our serpent friends have dressed up for the occasion," said Donald. I looked closer and saw that all of the snakes had red ribbons tied around them. "Those ribbons aren't just to make them look pretty. It'll be your job to remove every last one of them. The winner is the one with the most bows at the end."

"You can't be serious?" said Bruiser.

"Oh, come on, Joe," said Ronald. "Surely the star of Snakes on a Crane isn't actually scared of snakes?"

Bruiser's nostrils flared at this. "Those were CGI snakes," he snapped. "And I never said I was scared, did I? But ... I mean ... they're not

166

poisonous, are they?"

"Noooooo, of course not," said Donald, before turning to his partner. "Are they?"

"Not if you don't let them bite you," Ronald replied. "Any more questions? No. Good. OK, on three… GO!"

Zizi sprung into the pool and went straight to work, untying a ribbon from a cobra. Bruiser, however, didn't move an inch.

"Cam on, Joe," shouted Lexi, putting on a cockney accent. "You ain't gonna let that lil gel show you up are ya, son? Get in there!"

Despite Lexi's mocking, Bruiser stayed frozen to the spot.

Zizi, meanwhile, seemed to be removing ribbons with ease. She was even taking time to pet the snakes as she went.

Ronald and Donald frowned at each other as they watched Zizi's effortless progress. "She sure got over her fear of snakes pretty fast," muttered Ronald.

"Speaking of snake phobias…" said Donald, casting a glance at Bruiser, who hadn't so much as dipped a toe in the water.

It was just a matter of time before Zizi secured victory, untying the last of the ribbons from a water snake. Lexi and I cheered as she raised her arms in celebration.

Suddenly everyone watching drew a sharp intake of breath.

"What's wrong?" said Zizi. She turned her head slowly to the left where a red-and-yellow snake was dangling in the air, its teeth locked firmly on her arm.

"That can't be good," she said, before passing out.

CHAPTER
TWENTY

Lexi and I rushed into the pool and grabbed hold of Zizi, dragging out her limp body. Thankfully the snake that had bitten her had detached itself, but the damage had been done.

Pierre rushed toward her, barking his little head off as Karen called for the doctor.

I stepped back as a gray-haired man pushed his way forward, carrying a brown satchel. He dumped it down next to Zizi and started rifling through it.

"Did anyone see the snake that bit her?" he asked.

"It was a red-and-yellow one," said Lexi.

"Is she going to be OK?" I asked.

"She'll be fine," said the doctor. "I just need to administer the correct antidote. Now give me some space." He removed a big green book from his bag entitled *Snake Bites and You: A Beginner's Guide* and started flicking through it.

As I stepped away I realized that all eyes were on Zizi. I glanced back toward the path to Milo's camp.

This was it. Now or never.

It felt wrong leaving Zizi, but the doctor had just said she would be fine... Though I would have felt better about it if he'd found the page he was looking for.

I edged away from the crowd, clicked the Time-Out button, then turned and walked through the bushes. My walk quickly turned into a sprint, and I soon found myself at Milo's camp. I only just remembered to click the Time-Out device again before entering to make sure I took out their cameras too.

The camp was much like ours – except, of

course, for the bathroom, showers and bits of debris from what were presumably other Milo-related projects.

I headed straight for the tents. The first looked like it was only being used by one person. I remembered Milo saying that he and Cruul were sharing, and I could also see some of Bruiser's T-shirts lying all over the place with slogans like **COCKNEYS KICK HARDER** and **WHATCHOO LOOKIN' AT?**

I tried the other tent. One of the compartments was already open, and I recognized Milo's puffer jacket. I opened Cruul's side. It was easily the neatest of the three. All his clothes were folded and his sleeping bag was straightened.

It was only then that I realized I had no idea what I was looking for. I started rifling through his things, hoping to find a set of robes or maybe a handy guide entitled *How to Bring Back the Four Horsewomen of the Apocalypse.* But that wouldn't have been as surprising as what I did find.

Tucked among his T-shirts was a small pile

of paper. The first page was full of complicated legal terms, but I knew at once what it was. A management contract. I had signed one just like it when I'd joined Apocalips. But it wasn't my name on this one. It was Milo's.

Has Milo spoken to you yet? Mom's words rang out in my head. Surely Milo would never…

Someone behind me cleared their throat.

"Find what you were looking for?" asked Cruul.

CHAPTER TWENTY-ONE

"I'll take those," said Cruul, stepping forward and snatching the papers from my hands.

"Told ya I saw 'im sneakin' off," said Bruiser, who obviously hadn't been sent home yet.

"He must have slipped away when he heard the cameras were off again," said Karen, emerging through the trees along with the presenters and the rest of the cast and crew.

All eyes were fixed on me. Apart from Lexi and Milo's, who were staring at the ground.

"How's Zizi?" I croaked, my mouth feeling as dry as the sand beneath my feet.

"She's fine," said Cruul. "The antidote works

pretty fast. Though she'll be in no condition to continue on the show, so it's effectively a double elimination. But if you really cared I'm guessing you wouldn't have slunk off for a bit of burglary."

"Bloomin' thief!" yelled Bruiser. "They should kick 'im off the show."

"Look, Joe – a snake!" shouted Lexi.

Bruiser let out a high-pitched squeal, which sent Lexi into fits of laughter.

"You lil brat," said Bruiser. "They should send 'em both home, if yer ask me."

"No one did," snapped Cruul. "But I want to ask Sam something. What were you doing here?"

I was scrambling to think of an excuse, but I had nothing. Except the truth.

"I came to find out what you're really doing here on this show," I said. "Why do you have a contract with Milo's name on it?"

"What?" said Milo.

I grabbed the papers back from Cruul and waved them in my friend's face.

"Well…" said Cruul. "Oh, look, isn't it obvious?"

That caught me off guard. Was he actually about to admit to being here to bring back the Horsewomen?

"I came on this show to win," he said. "My career is in tatters, and I knew that even if I did win, it'd still be a long road back to where I'd been. When I heard that Milo was going to be here too, I saw a chance to speed things up. I'd heard the rumors about him going solo. I had my lawyer draw up a management contract just before I flew out. Sure it was a long shot, but I thought if I could convince him I was a changed man – and despite what you may believe, I truly am – then he might agree to take a shot on me. I know I can take him to the next level."

Everyone looked at Milo, but he just stood there saying nothing.

"Aren't you going to tell him to get lost?" I asked.

"Sam … please … not now," said Milo.

"What?" I said. "You're not seriously thinking…"

"Why wouldn't 'e?" butted in Bruiser. "Cruul's a good guy. Not like you. You should get the boot for this."

"Now, now, I don't think there's any need for that," insisted Cruul. "After all, who can blame Sammy for his mistrust? But really, there's no harm done. I'm sure if he were to apologize then we could all just draw a line under this sorry incident and move on."

"Apologize?" I said, almost spitting the word at him. "To you? You've got to be kidding."

"Seems fair enough to me," said Ronald.

"And me," said Donald. "Sam, either you apologize to Nigel or you're off the show."

I couldn't believe this. I was being asked to say sorry to the man who had almost helped bring about the Apocalypse.

I looked over at Milo, but he was busy staring at the ground. I turned to Lexi. She gave me the tiniest of nods. As much as I hated to admit it, she was right. I had no choice.

"Sorry," I muttered.

"What?" asked Cruul. "I didn't quite catch that."

"I said: **SORRY!**"

"Ah, there it is," he said. "Well, then. I think it's time that Team Ellipsis returned to their *own* camp now, don't you?"

Seething, I turned to walk away. As I reached the edge of their camp, I took one last look over my shoulder. Cruul, a thin smile etched on his face, winked at me.

Whatever it took, and whatever he was up to, I was going to stop that man.

CHAPTER TWENTY-TWO

Later that evening Lexi and I sat in silence, eating cold baked beans from a can. Our hamper had been taken away as a punishment for my expedition, and someone had even gone to the trouble of removing the remaining fruit from our camp.

"Well, that was a fun day," said Lexi, finishing the last of her can.

"Yeah," I said.

"You want me to do the next challenge?" she asked.

Tomorrow was the second Golden Challenge. It was match point for our team. If we won, the entire thing would be over – Cruul would have to leave the island. For that reason, I was sure he'd be doing the challenge himself.

"No," I said. "Cruul's mine."

It was true that I wanted to take on Cruul, but I had other reasons too. The challenges seemed to be getting increasingly dangerous, and Lexi had already done more than her share. If I let her volunteer again I'd basically be asking her to sacrifice herself for me, and there was no way I was doing that. Especially after what had happened with Steve.

Steve – the lead singer and only non-Horsewoman in Apocalips – had saved my life. If it hadn't been for him, I would have met the same fate as the Horsewomen that day at Hyde Park and been sucked into the void. Instead, Steve was. It haunted me still, and it made me realize I didn't want people putting themselves in harm's way to protect me anymore.

Lexi didn't seem convinced. "You might be better off saving yourself for the next Elimination Challenge," she said. "You do know that clips of you getting hit in the face by a fish probably aren't going to save you from that?"

"Yeah," I said. "But if I win, there won't be an Elimination Challenge."

"*If* you win," she agreed. "I don't mind doing them, you know. It takes my mind off…" Lexi's voice trailed off.

"What?" I asked.

"Nothing," she said.

Suddenly our conversation with our parents came to the front of my mind. "How come you were skipping judo?" I asked.

"What?" she said, the question catching her off guard. "Oh… I dunno…"

I thought I knew why. "You've got the Judo World Championships next year," I said. "And you're still doing karate and tae kwon do. And all three of your coaches are still expecting you to go to the Olympics, right? In three different sports?"

Lexi gave a shrug. "Yeah … well…" she said.

"It's a lot of pressure," I said. "And then you come here and pile even more on yourself."

Lexi turned away from me. Then her head started shaking. My first thought was that she was laughing because this seemed much likelier than what she was actually doing.

She was crying.

"Lexi?" I said, putting an arm around her shoulder.

"You're right," she mumbled. "It's too much. It's all too much."

The last time I had seen my sister cry was when she had found out that Steve had left Apocalips. Of course, Steve hadn't really left – he had been transported to an alternative dimension in front of my eyes as part of an elaborate plan to lure me into auditioning to join the band. And Lexi was under the band's mind control at the time. So there was other stuff going on, is what I'm saying. Still, I couldn't remember the last time I had seen her cry that wasn't Horsewomen-related.

"I… I thought you liked your classes," I said.

"I d-d-did," she sobbed. "I d-d-do."

"You're so good at them," I said.

"Yeah, that's the problem," she said, wiping snot off her nose. "They want me practicing all the time.

It's either that or school. That's all I do. I hardly see my friends or my family. Amy doesn't even bother calling me anymore because I'm always busy. I thought this show might give me a break, but there's just too much pressure. Either I'm trying to figure out what people at home are thinking about me, or I'm worrying about the next challenge…"

Lexi burst into tears again. I didn't say anything. I just pulled her toward me, and we sat there together, her head pressed against my chest.

After a while, she sat upright.

"Better?" I asked.

She nodded.

"You know, no one will think any less of you if you were to give up some of your practices," I said. "Or even all of them."

Lexi wiped her eyes. "I'll think about it," she said. "But right now I'm going to go to bed. You probably should too."

I had considered sneaking out to look for the hooded figures again, but there was an inflection in Lexi's last sentence that made it sound like she thought that would be a bad move. Given how the day had gone so far, she was probably right.

"Just make sure you win," she said as she pulled open the zip to her tent. "I've had enough of this place. Can't believe I cried on TV. Ugh."

CHAPTER TWENTY-THREE

APOCALYPSE INTELLIGENCE AGENCY

AIA

Voice: That was quite an emotional moment with your sister last night.

Sam: [Nods]

Voice: You don't want to talk about it?

Sam: Why would I want to do that? It was private.

Voice: [Pause] You are aware this is a reality TV show?

Sam: That doesn't mean I have to tell you about everything I'm thinking or every emotion I have.

Voice: [Longer pause] Seriously, have you ever even watched one of these shows?

The following day my prediction came true. Cruul volunteered for the challenge.

The trek into the jungle was the farthest we had gone yet. By the time we came to a stop, the forest was so dense you could barely make out the sky.

"For most of us this is as far as we go," said Donald. "But for Sam and Nigel this is just the beginning of their journey."

"For the second Golden Challenge," continued Ronald, "the two of you will embark upon a quest deep into the heart of the jungle, to find the tree that stands alone. Find the Golden Artifact hidden within, bring it back here, and you've won. It's as simple as that."

"Not quite," said Ronald. "For patrolling the forest is none other than **EL DEMONIO!**"

"El De-what-now?" asked Milo.

"**EL DEMONIO!**" boomed Donald. "The most fearsome beast to ever roam the earth. Next to him, the *Tyrannosaurus rex* would seem like a fluffy little poodle."

"What is El Demonio exactly?" I asked.

This drew knowing smiles on the faces of the two presenters. "Oh, don't worry, you'll know when you see him."

"Two more things," put in Ronald. "You'll both be provided with backpacks, containing provisions. You probably won't need them, but just in case El Demonio gives you more trouble than expected, at least you won't go hungry. Now since it's far too unsafe for us to follow you past this point, we'll be filming you remotely."

We all looked up to see a small drone, not much bigger than a pigeon, hovering in the air. It made a faint buzzing sound, a bit like an electric toothbrush.

"Hang on," I said. "It's too unsafe for you, but not for us?"

"Oh no," said Donald. "It's totally unsafe for you too, but it's your challenge. No point in us all risking our lives."

I couldn't help but frown as I slipped on the backpack handed to me by one of the crew. By the sounds of it, this challenge was shaping up to be just as dangerous as the others. Mom shouting at the producers clearly hadn't made any difference.

"OK," I said. "Let's get this over with."

"That's the spirit, Sam," said Ronald. "Nigel, are you ready?"

"Coming," he said. "Be with you in a—

OWW!"

"What's wrong?" asked Donald.

"My ankle," said Nigel, wincing in pain. "Think I've sprained it on a log. I'll be fine, though. I'll just have to walk it off."

Ronald and Donald exchanged worried looks. "Nigel, you can't compete," said Donald.

"Donald's right," said Ronald. "You'll have to let the doctor look at that."

A couple of crew members rushed over to help Nigel hop back the way we had come.

"He's faking it," muttered Lexi.

"How can you tell?" I asked.

"Because there was no log," she said.

I had a quick look around. She was right. I couldn't see any logs nearby, either.

Lexi's face suddenly lit up. She turned to Ronald and Donald. "Hey, does that mean they forfeit? Does Sam win?"

"No chance," said Ronald. "The Golden Challenge must be completed. Team Accelerate will have to pick someone else to take part."

All heads turned to Milo.

"I'll consult with the rest of my team, shall I?" he said, rolling his eyes. "Fine, I'll do it."

"Ronald, you know what this means?" said Donald, his eyes lighting up.

"I sure do, Donald," he replied. "It's **BEST FRIEND VERSUS BEST FRIEND!**"

CHAPTER TWENTY-FOUR

AIA
APOCALYPSE INTELLIGENCE AGENCY

As the drone buzzed above, Milo and I made our way deeper into the jungle, following the vague but ominous directions given to us by Ronald and Donald before we set out.

"*Straight on until you find the tree that stands alone,*" repeated Milo. "*Or until El Demonio finds you.*"

Our trip through the jungle with the rest of the group had been full of noise – rivers babbling, birds chirping, frogs croaking and monkeys screeching. But now all those sounds faded away until the only thing you could hear was our footsteps crackling on twigs and leaves, and the low hum from the drone.

"This is creeping me out," I said.

"I know what you mean," said Milo. "This place isn't right."

For a moment I had forgotten I was still angry with him. Why hadn't he just come straight out and said there was no way he'd ever sign with Cruul? The only reason I could think was that he was actually giving it some thought.

Like Lexi I just wanted the show to be over. This was our chance. All Milo had to do was let me win. Before yesterday I would have been sure that he understood this, but now I didn't know where his head was at. I couldn't very well ask him to throw the challenge. At best I'd be disqualified. At worst we'd both get the boot. And then all the pressure would be on Lexi's shoulders, which was the last thing I wanted to burden her with.

But I still wanted to make sure we were on the same page, at least for this. I had to send him some kind of signal.

"Why do you keep winking at me?" asked Milo as we stepped into a large clearing.

"Er … because… Wait, don't move!" I said,

pressing an arm against his chest. "What's that over there?"

Milo followed my gaze. "Oh…"

"Is that some kind of pig?" I asked.

"A boar by the looks of it," said Milo. "The tiniest boar I've ever seen."

Milo wasn't exaggerating. The boar could only have been about one and a half feet tall with tiny tusks. And he was covered in fluffy dark brown hair, like he had just been through a tumble dryer. While I would never go so far myself, I could definitely imagine some people throwing around the word cute to describe him.

"You have to admit, that is pretty cute," said Milo.

"Milo, look what's behind him," I said.

In the middle of the clearing stood a solitary tree. Its trunk was as wide as a car and seemed to spiral all the way up to the clouds.

"That'll be the tree that stands alone then," said Milo. "But you don't think that little guy is—"

"El Demonio?" I laughed. "Don't be silly. Look at the size of him. He's harmless… He's … He's charging right at us. Why is he doing that?"

"I don't know," admitted Milo. "I suppose we could stand here and discuss it if you wanted. Or we could run."

We both bolted for it, heading back the way we had come. The boar's squealing was getting louder and louder as he pursued us through the undergrowth.

"He's getting closer," I shouted. Then, maybe it was the adrenaline, but something popped into my head. "Milo?"

"What?" he shouted back.

"We got to speak to our parents after the last Golden Challenge!" I yelled.

"That's nice!"

"Mom asked if you had spoken to me yet!" I bellowed. "What was she talking about?"

"For crying out loud, Sam!" screamed Milo.

"We're getting chased through a jungle by a psychotic pig. Do you really think now is the time?"

"Sorry! You're right. What are we going to do?"

"We should split up," he cried. "It can't chase both of us at once. Look, there's a fork in the path up ahead. I'll go left, you go right. One of us should be able to double back and get the artifact."

I practically skidded down the path. Then I realized what he had just said. Milo was planning on getting the artifact. Surely he knew he had to lose? I looked around, but he had already gone.

What was he doing? Now I had to *actually* win.

I turned again, cutting through a bush and running back toward the lone tree. I couldn't hear the boar squealing anymore. I looked over my shoulder but saw no sign of him. Had he gone after Milo? Just as I began to worry about my best friend, I tripped and went tumbling to the forest floor. I sat up and turned to see what I had stumbled over snorting back at me.

Up close the boar did not look cute at all.

There was a look of viciousness about him that I hadn't seen since Vicky Heatherstone, and his tusks looked as sharp as knives.

"Nice boar," I said as he stared menacingly at me, grinding his hooves into the dirt. Slowly and without breaking eye contact I tried to get to my feet. I was halfway up when the pig let out an almighty scream that was enough to knock me back to the ground. He was toying with me. My only chance was to run for it.

"**WHAT'S THAT?**" I yelled, pointing into the bush.

The boar swung his head to look. Sometimes the simplest tricks work the best.

Seconds later I heard another screech. I didn't speak boar, but I could guess El Demonio wasn't pleased. I didn't look back as I shot through the jungle, eventually bursting into the clearing.

There was no sign of Milo as I sprinted for the tree. But with the world's angriest pig hot on my tail there wasn't much time to worry about that. I made a quick check around the base of the tree, then raised my head. About thirty feet up I could see a little nook in the trunk. Could that be where the artifact was hidden? There was only one way to find out – I'd have to climb. This decision was made a lot easier by the fact that El Demonio had reappeared and was charging toward me like a pig scorned.

I grabbed hold of the nearest branch and started scrambling up the tree, just as El Demonio struck the trunk at full speed. I felt a shudder as the tree shook with the collision, but somehow I managed to hang on.

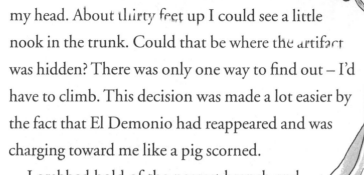

The boar began circling the base, grunting furiously up at me. Ignoring him, I continued to climb. After a few careful minutes I reached the hole and put my hand inside.

Nothing.

I moaned in frustration. Suddenly I saw something appear at my side and cried out in fright as I momentarily lost my footing. For a second I thought it was El Demonio himself, a flying boar come to finish me off. Then I realized that it was the drone, zooming in closer to get a better look.

Once I had regained my balance it occurred to me that I now had two big problems. One was finding the artifact. The other was getting down from this tree alive. I had no idea how I was going to do either.

"Hey! Looking for this?"

I gazed down as Milo stepped into the clearing. He was holding something in the air. Something golden. I couldn't make out what it was exactly, but I knew it had to be the artifact.

"Where did you get that?" I shouted.

"From the tree," Milo called back. "It was in that hole right by you."

I couldn't believe it. So while I had been tripping over boars, Milo had had a clear run to retrieve the artifact.

"I was heading back, but then I heard you cry out," he said.

I wanted to shout at him, but I couldn't even find the words.

Then Milo spoke again. "Look, he's not moving."

He was right. Despite now having a far easier target in Milo, El Demonio was still grunting in my direction. The pig wasn't remotely interested in anyone but me.

"Go away, you pest!" I shouted.

Milo approached the boar with caution, but there was really no need. "Clearly it's you he wants," said Milo. "Maybe he fancies you."

"Well, obviously I'm flattered," I said. "But I'm really not interested."

"What do you have that I don't?" muttered Milo.

"A killer smile?" I suggested. "A winning personality? Good looks?"

"No, none of those," said Milo, shaking his head. "Of course … the bags! What's in yours?"

Gripping the branch tight with one hand, I slipped off my backpack and unzipped it. I almost fell out of the tree anyway when I saw what was inside.

"It's full of meat," I shouted. "Sausages, burgers, there's even some steaks!"

Milo unzipped his own bag. "I've just got some bottled water and a few protein bars."

"So that's why he's chasing me," I said. "He can smell the meat."

"It was on your back," said Milo. "Couldn't you smell it too?"

"I… Well… I haven't exactly been smelling my best lately," I admitted. "We don't all have showers in our camp."

"Right," said Milo. "Well, chuck your bag down and we can get out of here."

"Gladly," I said, flinging the backpack as far as I could. It landed with a meaty splat somewhere in the jungle. With a triumphant snort, El Demonio disappeared after it, allowing me to climb down.

As I reached the bottom Milo held out his hand to help me, but I refused it.

"What's wrong?" he asked.

"What's wrong?" I repeated. "Someone just tried

to get me killed."

"We need to get to the bottom of this," said Milo.

"What, like how we got to the bottom of what happened to Lexi's barrel?" I snapped. "Still, I suppose it worked out for you."

"What are you talking about?" asked Milo.

"Well, you won, didn't you?" I said. "Cheating didn't work with Lexi, but it worked this time."

Milo frowned. "You think I *knew* about it?"

"I don't know what you know these days." I shrugged. "But I do know you're best pals with Cruul."

Milo blushed and looked away.

I could see that the drone was capturing all of this on film, but by this point I didn't care.

"He's going to be your new manager, isn't he?" I said. "Hang on, is *that* why you sent me to your camp? So I'd find the contract and you wouldn't have to break it to me yourself."

"What?" Milo said. "I didn't tell you to go to our camp."

"Not in so many words," I said. "But it was obvious what you meant."

Milo shook his head. "I think being on this island's messing with your head," he said, walking away.

"Yeah, well, we would have been going home right now if you hadn't taken the artifact."

Milo stopped and turned around. He held out his palm to show me the artifact.

It was a little golden insect of some kind. Milo opened his mouth to say something but seemed to think better of it. Then he turned on his heel and stormed off.

"I hope you and your mate Nigel enjoy your prize, because it's the last one you'll be winning!" I shouted after him.

CHAPTER TWENTY-FIVE

Voice: Sam, we can only apologize for what happened.

Sam: Someone tried to kill me!

Voice: That's a bit over the top. The boar was only interested in the food. You would have been fine. Probably.

Sam: Well, someone definitely tried to kill Lexi.

Voice: We've found no evidence to support that. It looks like it was just a faulty barrel.

Sam: And Zizi? She was bitten by a snake.

Voice: Yes, well, snakes do that kind of thing. We were under the impression that all the snakes in the pool had had their venom removed. But due to

an unfortunate admin error—

Sam: It's getting ridiculous.

Voice: We understand your concerns, Sam, and will endeavor to make sure that the next event is much safer.

Sam: Good!

We got our first taste of rain that night. And when I say rain, I'm not talking about the sort of annoying drizzle I was used to back home. This rain was like being under attack by the skies themselves. There was no chance of another trip into the jungle tonight. Lexi and I had taken shelter in my tent, and our mood matched the weather.

"I can't believe you flipped out on Milo," said Lexi. "He was so upset when he got back. I've never seen him like that before."

"Yeah, well, he's changed, hasn't he?" I said.

"Milo hasn't changed," she said. "You're the one who's turned into an idiot."

"Me?" I said in disbelief. "He's the one signing

up with Cruul."

Lexi laughed. "Of course he's not."

"How do you know that?" I asked.

"Because there's no way," she said.

"So why didn't he turn Cruul down on the spot?" I said.

"Probably because things were awkward enough thanks to you without Milo embarrassing Cruul in front of everyone," she said.

Oh. That did actually make some sense.

"I am a bit of an idiot, aren't I?" I said.

"A little," she said. "You'd better apologize to him."

"I will." I sighed.

The weather had cleared up by the following morning and thoughts returned to the next Elimination Challenge. It was the waiting around that was always the worst part. It didn't get any better knowing that this time I was definitely going to be nominated. There wasn't much I could do to prepare, but I did at least consider how I was going to pass the Time-Out device to Lexi if I lost the challenge. I figured I could probably slip it into her hand while giving her a goodbye hug. I tried not to think too hard about how much it was going to hurt to pull it out of my hair.

Lexi spent most of the day in the diary shed, which was unusual for her. Knowing Lexi, she probably had a lot bottled up and had finally decided to release some of it. I decided not to ask her about it when she came back.

It was almost a relief when it was time for the challenge. On the way to the cave, Lexi bombarded me with tips on how to defend myself, should the need arise. She was just explaining the finer points of flying kicks as we entered the chamber.

"Height is crucial, so you'll really want to push off with your knees and…" said Lexi, trailing off as we realized that the only other people here were Milo and Cruul. It wasn't unusual for Ronald and Donald to be absent, but there were normally crew around setting things up.

I glanced over at Milo. I wanted to apologize but

not with Cruul there.

"All right?" I asked him as we took our seats.

Milo grunted in reply, which resulted in a thin smile creeping across the face of Cruul.

"Oh dear," he said. "Not speaking?"

"Be quiet," I said.

"Yeah, be quiet," said Lexi. "Where is everyone, anyway?"

"There was some kind of problem with their equipment," said Milo. "I offered to take a look, but they said it was fine."

Wow. A technical fault that wasn't *my* fault. We sat in silence for a couple of minutes.

"Keeping out of trouble?" asked Cruul finally.

"Are *you*?" I said.

"Of course. I'm a reformed character now, remember," he said, smiling that thin smile of his.

"How's your ankle?" asked Lexi sarcastically.

"Oh yes, much better, thank you," said Cruul. "How's your mom and dad?"

In another lifetime Nigel Cruul had been the manager of our parents' band, **2-Incredible**, a fact that sent a shiver down my spine whenever I thought about it.

"Don't you bring up our parents," warned Lexi. "If you think my mom throws a mean punch, you haven't seen anything yet."

Cruul smiled wearily, giving his jaw a thoughtful rub as he did so. "I imagine they're not best pleased right now."

Lexi and I looked at each other in confusion. "About what?" I asked.

"Having to find a new member for Aftermath," he said. "Of course, I know better than anyone about the pains of having to find replacements."

"Replacements?" I said. "Who's leaving Aftermath?"

Cruul sighed. "Milo, obviously. That's why he turned down my offer. All the gossip sites figured he was about to announce he's going solo when really he's getting out of the industry altogether."

Milo scowled at Cruul. "That's not why I turned you down," he said. "And I asked you not to say anything…"

Cruul waved him away. "Sammy was going to find out," he said. "And besides, I thought he was your best friend. Shouldn't he have been the first person you told?" Cruul paused. "Ohhh, that's right, I forgot. It was Sammy who put the band together in the first place, wasn't it? So it's kind of his band in a way. Yes, I can see now why that would be difficult. Darn. I shouldn't have said anything."

"You're quitting the band?" I said.

As Milo opened his mouth to reply, the chamber suddenly started filling up. Ronald and Donald made their way to the stage while the crew quickly got their cameras set up, directed by the ever-stressed Karen.

"Sorry for the delay, everyone," she said. "Technical problems. All fixed now, but we'll have to speed things up since we're supposed to be going out live right now. Cameras rolling? Let's do this."

"Hello and welcome," said Donald. "Sorry for the late start, but we're all good now and ready to announce the contestants for today's Elimination Challenge. We're down to the final four. So without further ado, the person who received the most number of votes to be eliminated from Team Accelerate is… Nigel!"

I watched Cruul join the hosts on the stage, but all I could think about was what I had just heard. Milo was quitting Aftermath? But being in the band was his dream. And he was so talented. What reason could he possibly have to leave?

"And joining Nigel today from Team Ellipsis is…" announced Ronald.

This must have been what my mom had meant when she asked if Milo had spoken to me yet. But Cruul had a point, I should have been one of the first to know about it, not the last.

"…Lexi!"

To have to hear it from Nigel Cruul of all people. What was Milo thinking? And—

I looked up. "Wait … did he just say Lexi?"

CHAPTER TWENTY-SIX

My head was spinning. There had to be some mistake. After all that had happened, how could the public vote for Lexi over me?

Lexi was grinning sheepishly. "Don't get mad," she said. "But I might have spent most of today inside the diary shed saying offensive things to get people to vote for me."

"Like what?" I said.

"Oh, you know." She shrugged. "Dogs and cats are both terrible. Aftermath's music stinks. I even weighed in on which were the best Star Wars movies."

"Come on, Lexi," said Ronald. "We're in a rush."

"Why would you do that?" I asked.

Lexi leaned in and put her hands over our mics. "Because it needs to be you that makes it to the end," she whispered. "If the Horsewomen come back, you need to be here to stop them."

Lexi let go of the mics and got to her feet. "Don't worry," she said. "I've got it. Cruul's going down."

This didn't feel right. I had broken into Cruul's tent *and* fallen out with my best friend, one of the biggest pop stars around. Surely none of the things Lexi had said could be worse than that? The show was starting to feel like another rigged contest in my favor. In my head I could hear Zizi calling me the Chosen One.

I was still mulling things over as I followed the others outside toward an open-air truck. Once we'd all crammed in, the truck hurtled down the beach toward an expanse of grass.

The truck came to a stop, and we all climbed out. Parked next to us were two quad bikes.

Lexi let out a squeal of delight. "**NO WAY!**"

"Oh, for heaven's sake," said Cruul. "Another race?"

"That's right, Nigel, another race!" said a gleeful Donald. "Except this one—"

"Let me guess, it's unlike the others?" Cruul yawned.

"Well … yes," said Donald, looking a little annoyed. "But perhaps not in the way you'd expect. It's a real race. No gimmicks, no creatures and no chance of one of you being killed."

"Since there seems to be a rumor going around that we're trying to bump you all off," said Ronald with a nervous laugh.

The presenters explained the rules. The track was basically a circuit around the grass, the start and finish being where the two vehicles were parked. Lexi had already claimed one of the bikes and was admiring it with the same giddiness as the time she spotted Jason Statham in the supermarket.

"This is completely unfair," complained Cruul. "I'm a full-grown man, and she's an eleven-year-old girl. What about the weight difference?"

"You'll be putting on even more weight soon,"

said Lexi. "From all my dirt you're about to be eating."

"Yes, very good," said Cruul drily.

"Sorry, Nigel, but we only have the two bikes," said Ronald. "So it's that, or you walk."

Cruul sighed. "Very well."

He mounted his bike, and they both put on their helmets.

"Good luck, Lexi," I said.

"Don't need it, but thanks," she said.

Ronald and Donald counted down, the engines roared into life, and they were off.

Buzzing like hornets, the bikes cut across the grass. As Cruul predicted, the advantage was Lexi's. After just a few seconds she had pulled three feet or so in front. Cruul had his foot to the floor, but it didn't seem to matter – there was no catching Lexi. As she turned the corner at the other end of the field I breathed a sigh of relief. Lexi was right. She had this.

"Isn't this exciting," said Ronald. "No deadly animals or gross things to eat or drink. Just two quad bikes driving about for a bit. Thrilling stuff."

"Live TV at its finest, mate," said Donald sarcastically. "You know half the audience will have switched over by now?"

"Only half?" said Ronald. "That's optimistic. Still, at least we're nice and safe now. Wouldn't want anyone to think we're out to get them."

I could feel their eyes burning holes in the side of my head as I watched Lexi pass the halfway point, a comfortable few bike lengths ahead of Cruul.

"Are they finished yet?" asked Donald.

"Almost," said Ronald as Lexi swerved around the final bend and into the home straight.

"Good," said Donald. "This is the most boring thing I've been involved in since that time we presented the National Pebble Collectors' Awards."

"I liked that," mumbled Ronald.

"Come on, Lexi!" I shouted as she approached the finish line. It was going to take something pretty epic going wrong to stop her now. Like her getting struck by lightning or Cruul's quad bike turning out to have a secret hyperdrive or—

KABOOOOOOM!

The back of Lexi's quad exploded, flipping it into the air.

Yes, something like that would do it.

CHAPTER TWENTY-SEVEN

AIA APOCALYPSE INTELLIGENCE AGENCY

I let out a shout as Lexi hit the grass with a thud. Without thinking, I found myself sprinting toward her. I barely even registered Cruul as his bike sped past, only realizing afterward that he must have come within an inch of hitting me. Crossing the field seemed to take forever. Finally I dropped to the ground beside her. Through the visor in Lexi's helmet I saw her blinking and relief poured through me.

"Are you all right?" I said. "Sorry, silly question. Where are you hurt?"

"Ahhh," she moaned. "It's my arm. I think I've broken it. What happened?"

"There was some kind of explosion on the back

of your bike," said Milo, hurrying over.

"Someone put a bomb on it?" I gasped.

"A mechanical fault seems more likely," said Milo, "but I don't really see how—"

"Why don't we leave that to the experts to figure out," said Ronald as a couple of crew members pulled us away. The doctor strode past, accompanied by a couple of large men carrying a stretcher.

"They got here pretty fast," noted Milo.

"We'll get you patched up in no time, Lexi," said Donald.

"Did I win?" she asked hopefully.

"Oh no, of course not, mate," said Ronald. "You flipped your quad bike and broke your arm. As impressive as that looks in a slow-motion replay, it's a terrible tactic for trying to win a race."

"Viewers at home should be able to see that replay on screen now, by the way," added Donald. "And we'll have it up on the website in a few minutes."

A smug-looking Nigel Cruul was sitting on his

quad bike, parked on the other side of the finish
line. Despite her broken arm, it was clear the
anguish on Lexi's face was from the realization that
she had lost. The medical crew lifted her onto the
stretcher. As they passed us, Lexi glanced at me.
In that single look she said everything that
needed to be said. I was on my
own now. It was up to me to
stop Cruul from winning.
No matter what.

But just to be
sure, Lexi shouted
out, "Avenge me,
Sam. **AVENGE
ME!**"

"Um… OK," I said.

There were potentially
only two challenges left – the
final Elimination Challenge tomorrow
and, provided I won that, the last Golden Challenge
the day after. Team Accelerate only had to win one
of those to win the show. I had to win both.

"Where's Lexi's bike?" Milo asked Ronald and Donald. "I'd like to take a look."

"Don't worry, we've already got our top guys investigating it," said Donald.

"Are these the same guys that have been investigating all the other 'accidents'?" I said.

"Not sure, could be," said Ronald.

"Are we still pretending that someone's not trying to kill our team?" I asked.

"Now, Sam, seriously, mate," said Donald. "No one's trying to kill you. I'll be the first to admit, you are on quite a run of bad luck at the moment, but you shouldn't go throwing around accusations like that."

"I suppose you think it was me," said Cruul, giving me a patronizing smile. "Maybe I put a bomb on her bike, is that it? Yes, even though it was Lexi who picked her bike, I suppose I somehow knew in advance which one she would go for. Is that your theory?"

As hard as I tried to think of an explanation, I had no reply for Cruul. I looked desperately to Milo, but all he offered was a brief shake of his head.

"Well, thanks for your help," I said, then walked away.

"Sam, wait!" said Milo.

"Oh, let him go!" Cruul laughed. "Let him enjoy his last night on the island by himself. We'll all be going home tomorrow after our team wins."

"We'll see, Cruul!" I shouted back.

"Yes, we will see," agreed Cruul.

"That's what I just said!" I yelled.

"Yes, but I'm saying we will see in a way that suggests we'll actually see that I'm right, not you," he said.

"Well, we'll see, won't we," I said.

"Yes, that's what I'm— Oh, whatever!" shouted Cruul.

It was strange arriving back at camp. Seeing both tents, it felt like everyone else might still be around. But after a few seconds it sunk in that I was completely alone. Well, completely alone in a reality TV sense. Bill was still there, filming me from a distance.

Feeling my stomach rumbling, I decided to get a fire together. It took much longer than before, probably because I had never done it all by myself. But finally I got a pretty decent campfire going, one of the few things I had managed successfully on this island.

"*Bon appetite*," I said out loud as I tucked into a can of beans.

Once I'd finished, I sat watching the flames jumping around, casting strange shapes on the sand. Every so often I glanced over toward the part of the beach where I had first seen one of the hooded figures.

I wish I had found a way to tell Milo about the night Lexi and I discovered that cave. If only I hadn't spent all my time arguing with my friend, he might have made sense of it all. The cave painting, the hooded figures, the fact Cruul and I were still on the show – I felt certain that they were all connected somehow.

Now that this was possibly my last night on the island, I knew I had to find those hooded figures before it was too late.

I went inside my tent, took off my mic and waited for the sounds of Bill packing up for the night. Once I could no longer hear anything, I grabbed Lexi's flashlight, pressed the button on the Time-Out device and slipped back out.

I headed for the jungle, switching on the flashlight only when I was sure there was no chance of anyone seeing it from the beach. I decided to try to find the cave again, since it had been close to where we had last seen the hooded figures. I thought I knew roughly how to get there.

I had been walking for about twenty minutes when I heard something up ahead. A twig snapping. I killed the flashlight and ducked behind a tree. Then I waited and watched, fearful that the sound of my own heart beating would be enough to give me away.

Nothing.

I was about to put it down to an animal when a cold hand reached from behind me and clamped itself over my mouth.

CHAPTER TWENTY-EIGHT

"Mmpf!" I tried to shout.

"Shh! You'll give us both away!"

I spun around. "Milo!"

"Seriously, will you shut up?"

"Sorry," I whispered. "What are you doing here?"

"It's Cruul," he said. "He's on the move. Now keep your flashlight switched off, that's how I saw you. We're lucky Cruul didn't. Come on … this way."

Milo shot off back into the jungle. Confused, I followed after him.

"Where's he going?" I asked, once I had caught up.

"I don't know," admitted Milo. "But someone just showed up at his tent—"

"I thought you were in the same tent," I interrupted, pushing past a leaf the size of my head.

"We were until Bruiser left, then it made sense for one of us to move," he said. "It was a bit harder then to keep an eye on him during the night, so I built an intruder alarm that would wake just me if anyone entered or left our camp. I told him it was for catching mosquitoes. It's actually quite clever. It's coconut based—"

"Milo!" I said.

"Sorry, so yeah, the alarm went. And I heard a guy's voice telling Cruul that they'd found it."

"Found what?" I said.

Milo stopped suddenly as if he had heard something. After a couple of seconds he started moving again. "I think they went this way," he said.

"Found what?" I repeated.

"I don't know," he said. "But whatever it was, Cruul seemed pretty excited. He left the tent immediately. And I started following."

"What about the cameras?" I said. "Won't you have been seen?"

"Unlikely," he said. "Remember those toilets I told you about? I built one of them on a blind spot and put a secret back door in the shed."

"So you mean they'll have you on camera going to the bathroom and not coming out again for ages?" I said.

"Yeah," said Milo. "Luckily Cruul's been doing a lot of cooking recently. And hour-long trips to the bathroom afterward are not uncommon…"

I tried to put the image that was conjuring up out of my mind. "Did you see who Cruul was with?" I asked.

Milo shook his head. "It was too dark," he said.

"And he was wearing robes. It could be the same guy you saw on the beach that night."

I quickly brought Milo up to speed on my and Lexi's other discoveries.

"Why didn't you tell me any of this?" he said, sounding annoyed.

"It hasn't exactly been easy to speak to you," I said defensively. "I couldn't just use the Time-Out button any time I liked without people noticing. And there were other things going on, like someone trying to bump off our team."

"Which I had nothing to do with," said Milo firmly.

"Obviously I know that," I said. "I'm sorry about what I said to you. It's just—"

"You thought I wasn't taking the mission seriously," said Milo. "You thought I was letting myself get taken in by Cruul. You thought I'd let him be my manager. You thought becoming famous had changed me."

There was no point in lying. "Yeah," I said.

"Well, you're right," he said.

"What?"

"Not about taking the mission seriously," he clarified. "Or about Cruul. But you're right, being in Aftermath has changed me. It never would have taken the old Milo this long to realize this entire show is rigged."

I almost tripped as we stepped over a stream. "You think the show's rigged too?"

"Has to be," he said. "How else do you explain you avoiding the Elimination Challenges? You broke into our tent and went off at me for winning the Golden Challenge."

Even though I agreed with him, it wasn't the most flattering thing to hear. "Well, I don't get why you didn't just lose," I said. "Then this would all be over."

"We don't know that," said Milo. "I didn't throw the challenge because we still had no idea what Cruul was up to. If the show had ended, we wouldn't have been able to complete the mission. We needed more time. I thought you'd understand that."

"But…" I began before trailing off. "But Lexi

told me she got people to vote for her by saying horrible things."

"She fought an alligator," said Milo. "They'd have to have been pretty bad for her to get voted ahead of you."

We stopped in a clearing where light from the full moon had turned the jungle an eerie silver.

"Great," Milo groaned, looking back and forth. "We've lost him."

"Milo, I'm sorry," I said. "I should have trusted you. Do you forgive me?"

"Yeah, you should have," agreed Milo. Then, after a pause, he added, "Course I forgive you, you muppet. It's being on this island, it messes with your head. Probably why I ended up telling Cruul about leaving the band."

"So you're really leaving?" I asked.

He nodded. "You mad?"

"Why would I be mad?" I asked.

Milo looked confused by the question. "Well, it's like Cruul said, this was your band in a way. You put us all together. I put off telling you because…

I dunno… I thought I'd be betraying you or something."

I grinned. "Now who's the muppet?" I asked. "I only put you guys together because I thought you all deserved a shot. And you're so talented I thought that's what you wanted too."

"It was … for a bit," he said. "But being on tour made me realize what it is I actually love – science and inventing stuff and actually having time to hang out with my best mate."

"I miss that too," I said. "Though if we want to hang out again, it's probably best we stop Cruul from bringing back the Four Horsewomen of the Apocalypse."

"But how are we going to find him? He could be any—" Milo broke off. In the moonlight I could see his eyes darting back and forth. I knew that look – he had something.

"What is it?" I asked.

"The cave," he said. "Do you remember where it is?"

"I think so," I said. "There was this stream…

I was heading that way when I bumped into you."

"We need to go there right now," he said.

"You think that's where Cruul is?"

"No…" he admitted. "But from what you've told me, I have a feeling it might reveal his whereabouts."

CHAPTER TWENTY-NINE

"That's it!" said Milo. "I know where he's going."

It had taken some time to find our way back to where Milo had jumped out on me, but once we got there it didn't take long to find the stream and the cave. In less than ten minutes we had found the gap in the wall that Lexi and I had squeezed out through. Only this time the gap was much wider. Not only had someone been here, but they must have taken a sledgehammer to the entrance. After switching the flashlight back on, Milo and I had entered the cave with caution, but whoever had been here had already left. And now we were staring up at the painting. Whatever Milo was seeing, though, I wasn't.

"I don't understand," I said. "All I can see are loads of people in hoods following the Horsewomen."

Milo took the flashlight from me, then pointed it toward an area on the wall with a gathering of hooded figures. Flowing between them was a river. He then swung the flashlight to another section, where some more figures appeared to be assembled around a tree. "Look familiar?" he said.

"Is that the river where Lexi won the first Golden Challenge?" I asked. "And, yeah, that's the tree from the second one, isn't it?"

"Exactly," he said. "This isn't just some drawings on a wall, it's a map."

"A map to what?" I asked.

"There are two more places where the figures – and I think it's safe to say these are Apocalytes – seem to converge," he said, pointing toward the volcano in the middle and what looked like a giant hole to the east. "Cruul was heading east, he must be heading toward that pit. How much do you want to bet that the final Golden Challenge is going to involve the volcano?"

I shook my head. "But there is no volcano," I said. "We would have seen it."

"We have," said Milo. "We see it every day, except that it's either dormant or extinct now. I'm guessing at the time these paintings were made, it was a lot more active."

"The mountain?" I asked.

"Right," he said. "Come on, we need to find Cruul."

As we hurried back out of the cave, Milo glanced up at the sky. "There's the North Star," he said, pointing at a gleaming dot in the sky. He turned ninety degrees clockwise. "So east is this way. It's a giant hole, we're bound to notice it."

We moved as fast as we could, pushing our way through the dense vegetation. We had been walking for about half an hour when suddenly Milo grabbed the flashlight and switched it off. I heard it too. A low humming noise.

"Where's it coming from?" I whispered.

"Up ahead," said Milo.

We stepped carefully toward the sound. The closer

we got, the louder the humming grew. Eventually we came to the edge of a valley and instantly saw the source of the noise.

Apocalytes. Dozens of them. Maybe as many as fifty. Standing around a giant pit, chanting.

"You hear that?" whispered Milo.

"The chanting?" I said. "Yeah."

"No, not that. Something else. Coming from the hole."

I listened carefully. There it was. A faint scream coming from somewhere beneath the earth.

"Who—" I began, before breaking off as I realized something must have changed within the pit. The screaming had ceased, and now several of the Apocalytes were rushing to help pull up a rope. After several minutes, a battered and bruised Cruul emerged. He could barely stand as two of the Apocalytes supported him while another untied the rope from his waist.

"I did it!" cried Cruul, sounding delirious. He raised his right arm in the air. Clutched in his fist was a solid-gold dagger.

"What's that for?" I whispered.

"No idea," said Milo. "But I don't like the thought of Nigel Cruul being armed."

As Cruul and the Apocalytes began to leave the valley, luckily in the opposite direction from where we were hiding, I turned to Milo. "We should get down into that hole and take a look around."

Milo shook his head. "There's no point. It looks like Cruul's got what he went for. And now I need to get back to camp before he does."

"What?" I said, horrified at the thought. "You can't go back there now. He's got a knife."

"If his plan was to kill us he could have done it a hundred ways by now," Milo reasoned.

"What *is* his plan then?" I asked.

"I don't know," said Milo. "But that's the third Golden Artifact found. And from the cave painting we pretty much know there's a fourth. You can guarantee that the final Golden Challenge will happen. Which is good news for you, I guess."

"How do you figure that?" I asked.

"Because it means that no matter what you do in tomorrow's Elimination Challenge, you'll definitely win," he said.

"But if that's true," I said. "Then that means—"

"Someone from the show is working with Cruul," he said. "Given how many of those hooded figures we saw, maybe everyone on the show is. We can't trust anyone until this is over."

"So what do we do?" I asked.

"We have to play along," said Milo. "Try and get a message to the **AIA**. But those artifacts must be

the key to this. And there's one more to go. What I
don't understand is this: it looks like they only
found out the location of the dagger tonight.
So that's what they must have been looking for.
But if they knew where the others were, why
build a whole reality show around them? Why
not just fetch the artifacts themselves?"

Milo was right. It didn't add up.

"There's one thing for sure, though," he said.
"We can't let anyone get their hands on that last
Golden Artifact."

CHAPTER THIRTY

AIA

APOCALYPSE INTELLIGENCE AGENCY

Voice: Sam, I don't understand. That coconut you've brought along looks nothing like Katy Perry.

Sam: Or was it Lady Gaga?

Voice: Sorry?

Sam: Taylor Swift! It looks like Taylor Swift!

Voice: Sam you're acting very str— Actually, you're right, it does a little. From a certain angle...

I wasn't optimistic that my message to send help at once would make it to the **AIA**. And I still didn't feel much better about the fact that Milo was alone with Cruul, who now possessed a dagger.

When the time for the Elimination Challenge came, I held my breath as I entered the cave. But there he was, sitting next to Cruul.

Cruul was slumped in his chair and looked like he had just run a marathon without having done any training. Since I wasn't supposed to know what he'd been up to last night, I realized it might be strange if I didn't ask him why he was in such a state.

"What happened to you?" I said.

Cruul slowly raised his head. "Oh … nothing. Just… I suppose my cooking does need a bit of work. Right, Milo?"

Milo smiled weakly but was saved from having to add anything when Ronald and Donald appeared on stage.

"Well, this might very well be it," said Ronald. "The final challenge. Unless, that is, our young friend Sam prevails, in which case the competition will be decided by a third Golden Challenge."

More like fourth, I thought. I caught Milo's gaze and could tell he was thinking the same thing.

"We all know the stakes," said Donald. "Now let's crack on. Sam, as the only remaining member of Team Ellipsis, up you come. And joining you, from Team Accelerate … it's Nigel."

"Try to sound a bit more surprised," said Cruul. It took him a few seconds to get to his feet, and he looked very wobbly as he took to the stage.

A table and chairs were placed in front of us, though this table was much longer than the one they used for the first challenge. So another eating challenge? Cruul didn't look like he could manage a slice of toast let alone whatever vile concoction the producers had come up with this time.

"In case you were wondering – it's not an eating challenge," said Ronald. "It's going to be much more explosive than that."

"An interesting choice of words there," noted Donald. "*Explosive?* Is that referring to the hostility we've seen between the two contestants? The rising tension that's been bubbling over throughout the series, that we've been expecting will go **KABOOM** at any moment?"

"Er … no, mate," said Ronald. "It's because the challenge is to disarm bombs."

"Bombs?" repeated Cruul. "For the first time in your careers are you actually being funny?"

"Meow!" said Donald, grinning. "That was harsh. But no, you heard right. Don't worry – of course these aren't real bombs. They won't kill you – honestly, Sam – but you will want to take a shower if you lose."

Two small devices, each the size of a shoebox, were placed at opposite ends of the table. They had colored wires sticking out of them, and in the middle of each was what looked like an inflated balloon. Attached to the side was a clock with the following display:

"And how exactly are we supposed to disarm these things?" asked Cruul. "Do we at least get clues?"

"Oh, right, yeah," said Ronald, slapping his forehead. He took a piece of paper from his pocket. "Glad you reminded me, I had completely forgotten about the riddles. Let's see… *Captain Thunderhooves, ten to one, twenty pounds to win.* Hang on, that's just one of my old betting slips. What have I done with the riddles? You got them, Donald?"

"Not me, mate," said Donald. "You were supposed to have them."

"Are you telling me you've lost them?" said Cruul with a heavy sigh.

"Um … in a manner of speaking…" said Ronald, looking apologetic. "I know there was something about a dove on one … and maybe a goblin or something… Ah, never mind. I'm sure two smart lads like you can figure it out."

"And what happens if neither of us do?" asked Cruul.

"Then you'll both need a wash," said Donald. "Oh, I see what you mean. Yes, the first person to disarm their bomb wins. Don't worry, we've got plenty of spares stored in the back if you both need more tries."

"Phew," said Cruul.

"Are you ready?" said Ronald. "Go!"

The clocks on the devices started to count down. Cruul and I quickly took our seats.

We had to cut wires. I had seen enough movies to know that, and the pair of clippers next to my bomb confirmed it. But that was as far as I got.

I looked over at Cruul. He had cut a red wire and nothing bad had happened. His clock still seemed to be counting down, though.

I was just about to cut the red wire when Ronald said, "Oh, we should have pointed out that no two bombs are the same, so I wouldn't recommend copying your neighbor on this particular challenge."

I pulled my hand back.

A minute had already gone by, and I was no closer to even knowing where to start. Meanwhile Cruul had cut a second wire, green this time. He turned my way, a thin smile on his face as if he was able to taste victory. But at least his clock continued to tick down.

I glanced over at Milo, who was giving me a strained look as if he knew what to do and was dying to tell me. It was the same look he used to get in class whenever I'd get asked a question I didn't know the answer to.

But how could he know this time? Surely even Milo couldn't figure out which random wires to cut on a bomb. I wasn't sure he could even see it that well from where he was sitting. Unless…

Unless it didn't matter which wires I cut.

Milo was certain I was going to win. If Cruul's plan required a fourth artifact then it meant the Golden Challenge had to take place. And the only way to get to the final Golden Challenge was for me to win. And the only way to be sure I'd win was to make sure it didn't matter what I did. Milo had been convincing last night, but now, with a bomb under my nose, doubts were creeping in. After everything that had happened, how could I know for certain that this wasn't a real bomb? The kind that could blow me to smithereens.

BOOOOOOOOOMMMM!

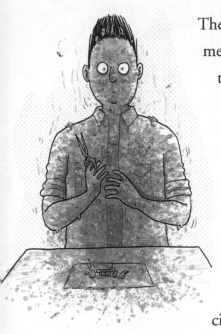

The explosion almost knocked me off my chair. Across the table, Nigel Cruul sat shaking. Well, I think it was Cruul. It was hard to be sure through all the layers of what looked and smelled like animal dung.

The room erupted into laughter. Under normal circumstances I'd have joined in, but my own counter showed I only had ten seconds left.

I had stopped trusting Milo once. I wasn't going to do it again.

I took a deep breath, closed my eyes and started cutting random wires.

I opened my eyes and breathed out. The clock had
stopped.

"We have a winner!" said Ronald.

My nerves were so shot I could barely process
what had happened. Cruul was being led out of the
cave by Karen. He had wiped some of the animal
droppings off his face and looked absolutely furious.
But I had a feeling that was only because of said
various animal droppings and not because of the
result itself. I wondered where they were taking him.

I was pretty sure he wouldn't be flying home any time soon.

"Well done, Sam," said Donald.

"Thanks," I said, though it was hard to take credit for something I knew was fixed.

"Yes, congratulations, Sam," said Ronald. "You've won the final Elimination Challenge. And now you and Milo will compete in the final Golden Challenge to find our winner. This will happen…"

"…right now!" finished Donald.

Milo and I stared blankly at the pair of them.

"Sorry, what?" I said.

"That's right!" announced a very excited Ronald. "We're not waiting another day to decide this."

"We're not?" I asked.

"No, we're not," confirmed Donald. "Ronald, why don't you tell them what the challenge involves?"

"Thanks, Donald," said Ronald. "Yes, of all the challenges this is the most arduous yet."

In a competition that had included zorbing with scorpions, fights with alligators and getting chased by a demonic boar, that was a worrying statement.

"I'm sure you've noticed –" continued Ronald – "the big mountain in the middle of this island?"

Milo and I nodded.

"Excellent," he said. "Well, the final artifact currently sits atop that mountain. Whichever one of you brings it back is our **End Games** champion."

So Milo was right – the mountain was the final challenge.

As we emerged from the cave a sharp, cold wind blew all around us, and the blackest clouds I had ever seen had appeared in the distance.

"A storm's coming," said Milo. "Looks like a bad one. We'll have to postpone the challenge."

"Ah, probably just a shower," said Donald.

"That's right," agreed Ronald. "We'll see you when you get back, yeah? We'll be watching." He pointed to the drone, which had just flown into view.

"Now we know this competition has really put a strain on your friendship," said Donald, giving us what I think was supposed to be a caring smile. "But the quicker you get back, the sooner your relationship can be mended."

I had almost forgotten that everyone still thought Milo and I weren't speaking.

"We all set?" asked Ronald. "All right, then. For the final time – three … two … one…"

After being handed raincoats – just as a precaution, Ronald insisted – we set off.

"Shouldn't we have equipment or something?" I asked Milo as the mountain loomed over us.

"On this show?" he replied.

"Good point."

We didn't talk much more after that as we concentrated on the terrain itself – a thin, rocky trail wrapping its way around the mountain like a python squeezing its prey. It would have been difficult enough to scale under normal circumstances, but the rain lashing into our faces added that extra dimension of misery. The drone was having an especially hard time of it, the wind blowing it all over the place as it tried to keep track of us.

We were about two thirds of the way up when a

gust of wind sent the drone flying past us. Without hesitation, Milo reached under his raincoat and ripped out his mic, then flung it over the side of the mountain. Not bothering to ask why, I did the same.

"When that thing comes back you need to disable it," he said.

I nodded. "Right." We waited for a moment while the drone readjusted itself. Like a drunken bee it swung its way toward us, until it was finally close enough for me to activate the Time-Out device. I pressed the button.

Nothing.

"What's happening?" asked Milo. "Why's it still up there?"

"I don't know," I said. "The Time-Out's not working. Maybe it's the rain or the battery has run out."

"Or maybe they're wise to it now," said Milo. "I guess we'll just have to do things the old-school way for this one."

Another gust caught the drone again, knocking it behind us this time. Milo reached down and picked up a round flat rock. With a backhanded motion he hurled it through the air, smacking the drone and sending it hurtling toward the ground.

"Good aim," I said, impressed.

"All the practice we did for the Catch Me Like a Frisbee music video finally paid off," said Milo. "Now, come on."

The closer we got to the summit, the narrower the trail became. We had to climb the last forty feet or so, scaling the rocks with just our bare hands. I tried to keep my head up, certain that if I looked down just for a second I'd quickly be joining the drone below. Finally, with scraped knees, bruised shins and bleeding palms, we made it.

With the rain still lashing down, we paused to get our breath back. Suddenly we heard a faint buzzing from somewhere above. At first I thought it was another drone, but the noise grew louder and then there it was – a plane. It tipped from side to side as it flew past, its altitude dropping the whole time. It looked to be heading toward the strip of grass where the quad bike challenge had taken place.

"What's it doing out in this weather?" asked Milo.

"Perhaps it's come to take Cruul home," I said, not really believing it. The plane looked similar in size to the one that had brought us to the island. "Or it could be the **AIA**. Maybe they got my message."

"Maybe," said Milo, not sounding convinced of either theory. "Let's get moving."

The summit of the mountain was rocky but largely flat. It didn't take us long to find the artifact. Embedded into the rock itself was a golden skull.

"Of course," said Milo, slapping his forehead. "I should have known."

Only Milo could spot a gold skull sticking out of the ground and get annoyed that he hadn't seen it coming. "What?" I asked.

"The artifacts," he said. "Gah, it's so obvious now. Remember what I told you about the Horsewomen back on the plane?"

I had to think for a second. "About them being Death, War, Famine and Pesticides," I said.

"Pestilence!" he shouted. "But yeah. So the first Golden Challenge – Lexi goes up against some very hungry alligators. The artifact is an empty plate. That's Famine. The second artifact, the insect, must be a locust – as in a plague of locusts. And if that boar that chased us doesn't qualify as a pest then I don't know what does. Next it's Nigel's secret challenge. Whatever happened down that pit, from the look of him he'd been through a war, and I'd say as symbols of war go, a dagger would do the job. And now we have a skull."

"Death," I said.

"Exactly. One for each of the Horsewomen. If these are what can bring the Horsewomen back then we've got no choice. We have to destroy that thing."

"Actually, I was thinking about this on the way up," I said.

Before I could explain further, Milo reached for the skull, but as his hand got close to it, he stopped.

"I can't touch it," he said.

"What do you mean?" I asked.

"I dunno. It's like there's a force field around it

or something. You try."

I reached down and effortlessly picked up the skull.

"Hmm," said Milo. "That's odd."

I turned the skull over in my hands. It felt cold and heavy, but mostly it just filled me with dread. "Hey," I said, a thought occurring to me. "If all the other challenges were related to the artifacts and to the Horsewomen in some way – Famine, Pestici— Pestilence, War – what's the Death part of this challenge?"

As soon as I had finished speaking the rock beneath us started shaking. Right where the skull had been resting, the ground started crumbling away.

"You had to ask!" yelled Milo.

We sprinted toward the edge of the summit. By the time we got there, most of the mountain peak had fallen away to reveal a crater filled with furious-looking molten lava. The volcano was neither dormant nor extinct. It was as awake as a volcano could possibly be.

I was about to start sliding down the rocks when I turned to see Milo, standing at the edge of the crater, staring into the lava.

"Come on," I shouted. "Let's go!"

"The skull!" he yelled back. "Throw it in! It's our only chance to destroy it."

"We can't," I said. "I'll explain later, but we have to go. Now!"

As I reached out to grab his hand, the ground beneath Milo's feet gave way, and he fell.

CHAPTER THIRTY-TWO

AIA APOCALYPSE INTELLIGENCE AGENCY

Voice: Sam! What happened? We lost audio and visual on you. Where's Milo?

Sam: He's... He's gone... The volcano...

Voice: [Pause] Why did you come to the diary shed? Why not go back to the cave?

Sam: Tired ... this was ... closest place...

Voice: Sam, did you... Did you get the artifact?

Sam: [Holds up skull]

Voice: He's got it. All right, Sam, just stay there. We're evacuating the island. Someone's coming to get you right now.

Sam: It's over? No... No more?

Voice: Yes, Sam. It's all over.

Moments later the diary shed door burst open, and several Apocalytes were standing there. Two of them grabbed hold of me and dragged me from the shed. Another snatched the skull from my hands, whatever force that had prevented Milo from touching it apparently lifted.

I put up no struggle as my hooded captors marched me through the jungle in the pouring rain. I didn't even bother trying to get a look at their faces. I had a pretty good idea who they were, and knew I'd find out for certain soon enough.

I'm not sure how long we walked for. It could have been ten minutes, or it could have been thirty. In front of me, in the distance, black smoke was billowing from the volcano. Wherever we were going though, I wasn't being evacuated.

Eventually they led me out into a large clearing. The area was marked by four massive standing stones, arranged in a square formation. All around the stones were little pink flowers. At first glance it reminded me a bit of Stonehenge, except with fewer stones and these ones were…

I gasped. They weren't just stones. They were heads. *Identical* heads. Huge stone carvings of the Horsewomen, all looking right at me.

And then I knew what the flowers were. They were heather. *Heatherstones.*

Dozens of Apocalytes emerged from the jungle, filling the spaces between the stones. The pair who had been my escort merged into line with the others. Then another stepped forward, giving me a slow clap.

"Congratulations," said Cruul, lowering his hood. "You won. I thought you might. Sorry about your friend. You know, for what it's worth, I actually quite liked him. He had talent. And he wasn't half as annoying as you. Still, given what's coming, it's probably best that he got out when he did."

"Why, what's coming?" I asked.

I stood my ground as Cruul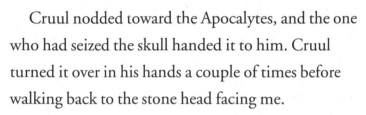
walked toward me, our eyes locked
on each other the entire time.

"I'm sure by now you've
guessed what's coming," he said.
"Or rather ... who."

Cruul nodded toward the Apocalytes, and the one
who had seized the skull handed it to him. Cruul
turned it over in his hands a couple of times before
walking back to the stone head facing me.

I looked around at the stones and realized that
embedded in the forehead of each Horsewoman was
one of the Golden Artifacts – the plate, the locust
and the dagger. And now the skull.

Cruul pressed it into what I knew had to be
Veronica's forehead.

I flung myself to the ground as
flames shot out of the eyes of
the Heatherstones, converging in
the center and quickly forming
a giant molten ball. I had seen
something like it once before –

when I had witnessed the Horsewomen, in their boy band guise, appear to obliterate Steve.

Only this time, four silhouettes began to appear in the flames, to wild cheers from the Apocalytes.

A girl, about the same age as me, emerged from the sphere. She was thin and pretty with long golden hair and a floor-length black dress. And she was riding a huge pale-green horse. Three identical girls followed after her, all on horseback.

"**Weeeeee're baaaaaaaaacck!**" said Veronica Heatherstone.

"Hello, Sam," said Veronica, in that deep voice of hers. It was one of the few ways you could tell the Horsewomen apart. "Did you miss us?"

"Not really," I said as the four dismounted from their menacing horses.

Veronica pouted. "Oh, Sam, that's not very nice. We missed you. We've thought about you every day. We've thought about little else in fact. Mostly about what we'd do to you when we saw you next."

"Where were you?" I asked, trying to buy time. If I knew anything about the Horsewomen, besides them being horrible and evil, it was that when given the chance to talk about themselves, they'd take it.

"Where you sent us," snapped Valerie. "The darkest dimension. A universe of pain and destruction with no hope for anyone or anything."

"It wasn't all good, though," added Violet. "They didn't have Netflix."

"And I haven't punched anything in months," snarled Vicky, always the most aggressive of the four. "Well, nothing with a face, anyway."

"But now we're back," said a gleeful Veronica. "And it feels goooood."

"But how?" I asked.

"Oh, Sam, you simple little idiot," said Veronica. "Did you really think that after centuries of planning and waiting that we wouldn't take out an insurance policy? Are you really that dumb?"

"The island," I said.

"Of course the island," she replied. "For millions of years this was our home. It was just the four of us, minding our own business, trying to come up with schemes to destroy the universe. We had finally managed to get rid of all those silly dinosaurs so we were on a bit of a roll. But then humans started slowing up. Humans were pretty dumb in those days, even dumber than they are now. We put up with them for a bit though, because they worshipped us like gods. They were the original Apocalytes, devoted to aiding us in bringing about the End of Days. Eventually, when the time was right, the Apocalytes left the island and joined the rest of the world, taking up key positions of power and helping us recruit even more loyal followers." She looked over at Cruul as she said this. He was grinning like a fool, while his fellow Apocalytes bowed their heads devotedly.

"We came up with the plan for Apocalips hundreds of years before boy bands were even invented," continued Veronica. "But the prophecy that warned of you concerned us. We needed a Plan B. So we concealed the island from the world and began feeding it a steady diet of ships and aircraft, building up a store of energy that could be used to return us to this dimension. And then destroy it."

She turned to face the volcano. More smoke than ever was billowing from it, and yellow lava was spurting out of the top as rain continued to lash down on the island. "Isn't it beautiful?" she said. "You've heard of supervolcanoes, yes?"

I nodded. Milo had told me about them before. Apparently there's this one in America, in Yellowstone Park, so big that if it went off it could trigger a new ice age.

"Well, this is like that," she said. "But a gazillion times worse. Imagine an explosion so powerful it would destroy space and time itself. I mean … doesn't that sound awesome?"

I didn't think it did, to be honest. But this all begged another question.

"Why didn't you just use that, instead of becoming a boy band?" I asked.

The Heatherstones rolled their eyes as if they couldn't be bothered dignifying this with a response. And then I remembered.

"Of course," I said. "You can't kill people yourselves. The ancient laws of the milliverse or something."

"Multiverse," snapped Valerie. "It's those ridiculous ancient laws of the multiverse."

"Yes," agreed Veronica. "There are always checks and balances to these things. You think you're so clever, Sam, but you don't know what it's like being us. We exist solely to bring about the Apocalypse, but you have no idea how difficult it is. We have all these ancient laws to deal with. Oh, we can't kill humans directly. But we *can* use the energy from love to rip a hole in the fabric of reality – just so long as a teenage boy doesn't sing 'Jingle Bells.' All these forces that hold us back. Cosmic red tape is what it is."

"So that's what the TV show was for?" I said. "And the challenges? The artifacts were just keys to bring you back?"

"Look at that, he's not completely dumb," said Vicky.

"I was smart enough to defeat you all, wasn't I?" I said.

Vicky's face went bright red. "Can I thump him now?" she asked.

"Soon, Vicky," said Veronica. "But this is the first time we've gotten to recap something in ages. Let's not ruin the moment."

"Fine," muttered Vicky, giving me the evil eye. Which, to be fair, is just a regular eye for her.

"Yes, the artifacts were the keys," said Veronica. "Boy bands love a good key change, after all. We decided to use some objects placed here thousands of years ago by the original Apocalytes. The island would reappear if ever we left this dimension, and Cruul was given detailed written instructions as to where to find them."

Cruul grinned at me. "They were in that pile of paper in my tent. I didn't even bother hiding them. I knew if I put a contract with Milo's name on it at the top, you'd never bother looking past the first page. If you had, you'd have found out where all the artifacts were. Well, except for Vicky's. She … ahem … never got around to writing hers down. Luckily we found the cave painting…"

"One artifact for each Horsewoman," continued Veronica. "Unfortunately only the four people responsible for our downfall could retrieve them. And each could only take a single one."

Four people most responsible for their downfall…
So that was me, Lexi, Milo and… I looked over at
Cruul, who was hanging his head in shame as the
Horsewomen glared at him.

"I get why we three were to blame," I said. "But
what did Cruul do? He tried to help you, didn't he?"

"Yeah, he tried," said Valerie. "But he failed.
Miserably."

"It was his job to keep you from the stage at
Hyde Park," said Vicky. "But he messed it up.
Didn't you, Nigel?"

"Y-y-yes," whimpered Cruul. "B-b-but I've
redeemed myself, haven't I? I brought you home."

"You did well," conceded Veronica. "As a reward, we will allow you to explain your plan to our friend Sam."

Vicky folded her arms and stamped her foot. "Not another recap!" she said. "When can we start blowing things up?"

"Soon," said Veronica. "Nigel, continue."

"Thank you," said Cruul, his face lighting up. "Um… Yes, so my plan … it was most intricate."

"It's your show," I said. "I'm guessing you own the production company. You've been making TV like this for years, so you knew how to manipulate the audience to vote exactly how you wanted. I mean, you could have just rigged the vote, but you're so arrogant you would have thought that unworthy of your skills. The challenges all went exactly the way you wanted. If someone had to be up for nomination then you showed the worst footage you could find to convince the public to vote for them. You didn't show me shouting at Milo or breaking into your tent because you wanted me here at the end. You needed me to retrieve the final artifact. And I imagine you were also looking forward to me having to listen to you tell me how clever you are."

Nigel's mouth was hanging wide open. "Well!" he said. "That's just absolutely unacceptable. After all the work I've put in, how dare you steal my thunder?"

"Every challenge was fixed," I continued. "Like the meat in my bag, or it not mattering which wire I cut on that bomb. We might have noticed that sooner except for Lexi's barrel in the first Golden Challenge. If you wanted her to win, why sabotage *her* barrel? That part doesn't fit."

Cruul's cheeks went a little pink. "It was a mistake. The hole was supposed to go in the barrel to the right."

"They told me left!" shouted a familiar voice. One of the figures lowered their hood to reveal a face covered in painful-looking purple blotches, marks I knew had been left there by angry scorpions.

"Betty?" I cried.

"Oh, don't look so surprised," she said. "I was a struggling actor going nowhere until my mistresses got me the Cliffhanger Road gig. It's no coincidence I got the boot after you got rid of them either, you know."

"I did not tell you left, I told you right," said an Apocalyte clutching a tablet.

"Karen?"

"Of course Karen," she said, pulling down her hood. "We're trying to organize an Apocalypse here, someone needs to keep on top of things."

"'ang on a minute," said another voice, in a thick East London accent. "You mean to tell me that I was supposed to be the one getting fed to those 'gators?"

"We all have to make sacrifices, Joe," said Betty, vigorously scratching her body as she spoke.

Joe Bruiser removed his hood, then looked over at me and smiled. "All right, sunshine? Surprised to see me again, are ya?"

"No," I said flatly. "I knew Cruul must have had help. Betty was a surprise. Karen maybe. But you would have been top of my list of people to sign up with the Horsewomen. You and Bo."

"Who told him I was here?" said Bo, taking off his hood. "I bet it was one of you One-Gens."

"One-Gens?" I asked.

"One-Generation Apocalytes," he said. "People that only signed up because they got something out of the deal. Whereas my family descends from the Original Apocalytes. I'm practically royalty."

"Good for you," I said.

"Well, I bet you didn't expect us," said Ronald as he and Donald stepped forward.

The Horsewomen looked at each other blankly.

"Sorry, who are you?" asked Violet.

The pair laughed nervously. "We're Ronald…"

"And Donald," said Donald.

"Ronald and Donald?" said Valerie.

They nodded.

"Well, that sounds annoying," she replied.

"We've been your faithful followers for years," said Ronald.

"So … we've met you before?" asked Vicky.

"Yes!" said Donald. "Many times. We swore allegiance to you, and you helped make us the nation's most beloved TV hosts."

"Oh yes, of course," said Veronica. "Now we remember. Yes... Ronald and... What was it again?"

"Donald."

"Donald!" said Veronica. "Right. Great to have you both on board."

As the pair perked up a little, Veronica gave the other Horsewomen a baffled shrug. Then she turned toward the crowd. "All right, the rest of you might as well reveal yourselves."

The remaining hoods were removed, revealing the faces of all the crew members. I had prepared myself for this, but seeing Bill the camera guy was still hard to take. And there was one person among the crowd that I hadn't seen coming. It was like a punch to the stomach.

"Hey, Sam!" said Zizi, giving me a wave.

CHAPTER THIRTY-FOUR

"Zizi?" I gasped. "What are you doing with them?"

"I just signed up," she said. "It's great, you get free robes. Look, they even made some for Pierre." She held up the pug, who looked even grumpier than usual.

"But why?" I asked.

"Because I'm fed up with doing boring reality shows," she said. "If I'm lucky I get to host things like *Britain's Next Top Trashman* or *Have I Got Newts for You*? But I want to act, and Nigel says the Horsewomen can make that happen!"

"We certainly can," said Veronica, smiling.

"Or be a DJ," Zizi added.

I pointed toward the volcano. "**BUT THEY'RE ABOUT TO DESTROY THE UNIVERSE!**" I shouted.

Zizi's face filled with disappointment. She turned to the Horsewomen. "I don't suppose we could delay the Apocalypse a bit? Just till I get a few gigs in?"

"Um … we'll have a think about that and get back to you, yeah?" said Valerie.

Zizi smiled, looking appeased by this.

Suddenly the ground shook for a few seconds.

"Enough of this nonsense," snapped Veronica. "There's not a lot of time. Bring us the girl."

The crowd parted to allow a pair of figures to walk through.

"Get off!" Lexi yelled as Bruiser shoved her toward me. Her broken arm was bandaged up, but poorly by the looks of things.

"Lexi!" I said. "You're still here."

"They took me after the race," she said. "Told me we were going to a medical tent. But it was a prison."

"You were in a trailer," said Bruiser. "'ardly a prison."

"You made me watch videos of Bo opening boxes all day," she said. "If that doesn't count as torture…"

"Serves yer right for all the bites and scratch marks yer've given me," Bruiser said.

"You'd have gotten worse if I didn't have a broken arm," said Lexi. She turned back to me. "Where's Milo?"

"Yes, where is the other one?" asked Veronica impatiently.

Cruul drew a finger across his neck. "Gone," he said. "Fell into the volcano."

Lexi gasped. "Sam? It's not true?"

"He's … in a better place now," I said quietly, choosing my words carefully. Lexi screwed up her face in confusion.

"He's dead?" roared Veronica. "You fool, Cruul! How could you let that happen?"

Cruul looked stunned, turning to the others for help. "Er … sorry, I don't…" he said. "What does it matter if he's dead? You're here now."

The Horsewomen looked ready to explode.

"You idiot, Cruul!" shouted Vicky. She pointed at the pulsating ball of fire, which was still floating in the air behind us. "Why do you think the portal is still there?"

Cruul could only offer a shrug. "I don't know," he said. "Because it looks cool?"

"You can't just travel between dimensions freely," said Violet. "Everyone knows that."

"There's always a cost," said Valerie.

Cruul gulped. "And what might that be?" he asked.

"The four who opened the portal, of course," said Veronica. "A trade. Us for them."

Cruul looked hurt. "You mean you were going to send me to the darkest dimension?"

"You were fine with the Apocalypse," I snapped. "What does it matter to you?"

"Better here than in there, to be fair," said Violet. "Nothing dies in that dimension. It's just constant pain and suffering forever. With giant flying bat-bear things. And no Netflix."

"And if the portal doesn't get its payment," said Veronica. "It takes it. With interest. It'll use the power we need to destroy the universe

277

to swallow this entire island instead. Ugh. This is ridiculous. Well, if we don't have all four of them, it looks like the Apocalypse will just have to wait. We need to leave at once."

The other three Horsewomen let out a collective "Awwww!" at this.

"I know, I know," said Veronica.

"There's a plane on standby," said Karen.

"Very well, let's go," said Veronica. "My hair's getting soaked in this rain."

Cruul was about to follow, when Vicky put a hand on his chest. "Not you," she said. "You've failed us once too often."

"But, Mistress…" Cruul started to plead, before Vicky shoved him to the ground.

Veronica was just about to mount her horse when she stopped and looked back. "You figured it all out, didn't you?" she said. "Cruul's plan."

"In the end, yeah," I said. "Together with Milo."

"Yet you still went through with it," she said, looking at me curiously. "You still brought back the final artifact. Why?"

I didn't reply, but my eyes drifted toward the portal. Veronica saw this. After a few moments she burst into laughter. "Oh, you hoped *he* would be with us, did you?"

The other three joined in her laughter. "You brought back the Four Horsewomen of the Apocalypse on the off chance that we'd bring Steve too?" said Valerie.

"Sorry to disappoint you," said Veronica, wiping a tear from her eye. "But we haven't seen that fool in a long time. He's probably living inside the digestive system of something too disgusting to imagine. Still, how noble."

I took one last glance at the portal. It had been a long shot, but I knew I'd had to try. If it hadn't been for Steve then it would have been me living in that misery. There was only one thing for it then. It had worked before; I had to hope it would work again. I cleared my throat and started singing: "**Dashing through the snow, in a one-horse open sleigh...**"

The Horsewomen froze. As I continued to sing, they clutched their ears before dropping to the ground and writhing around in agony.

Then they all burst out laughing again.

"Did you really think it'd be that easy this time?" sneered Veronica as the four of them got back on their feet. "Being sent to the darkest dimension did have some benefits. We've learned things. New powers beyond your comprehension. Like the ability to resist your terrible singing, for a start."

So much for Plan A.

"What now?" Lexi asked me.

"Lexi, it's going to be OK…" I whispered, my voice drifting off as I noticed Karen running through the rain toward the Horsewomen, waving her tablet.

"Mistresses!" shouted Karen. "The other boy. He's alive."

"What?" asked Veronica. "How?"

"He lied," said Karen, pointing an accusing finger at me as if that had been the worst thing anyone had done recently. "The drone we had following them had a self-recovery mechanism built in. It managed to capture this footage."

Her curiosity piqued, Veronica pressed her palm to the screen then swiped it to the left, projecting a huge floating image of me and Milo on the volcano. The video started to play from the point when the ground beneath Milo had given way.

It showed the moment I swung my arm, only just managing to grab Milo's hand. It had taken every ounce of strength I had to pull him back up, but somehow I had managed it. Veronica waved a finger in the air, fast-forwarding through the rest of the footage of us rushing back down the volcano.

"He's alive!" shouted Violet.

"Yay! There's still time to blow everything up!" said Vicky, clapping her hands in delight.

"Find him!" Veronica bellowed at the Apocalytes. But none of them moved. They were all busy pointing at the portal.

"What is it?" said Veronica, throwing her hands in the air as she turned around. Forming in the portal was a new silhouette. Moments later a man emerged.

"Steve!" shouted Lexi.

It was Steve, but you could be forgiven for not recognizing him. The last time I had seen him he was clean shaven, wearing a shirt and tie with a porkpie hat. The hat was gone, but the tie was now wrapped around his forehead, and he had a wild, bushy beard. He looked a lot more muscular than I remembered and for some reason he had a sword. His eyes were fierce, and there was no doubt that this was a Steve who had seen things no Steve should ever see.

"What are you doing here?" screamed Veronica. The portal had started pulsating violently, turning a bright green. "The portal only allows four to pass through it. Four. Not five. You're ruining everything again."

"Oh, I am so terribly sorry," said Steve. "Though I see you all brought your horses."

"Our horses are a part of us," said Valerie defensively. "They don't count toward the quota."

"Yeah, whatever," said Steve. "But I'm not going back in there. I just had to fight off a mutant meerkat."

"Oh, we'll see about that," said Vicky, rolling up her sleeves.

"Bring it on, *Warren*," said Steve, twirling his sword like some kind of boy band warrior. A boy-barian perhaps?

"Warren?" she scowled. "That's who you want, is it? Well, let's see what I can do."

Vicky began to morph into her former alias, her smooth skin becoming rugged, her pointy chin becoming chiseled. Then, about halfway through the transformation, the whole process stopped, leaving her in a grotesque state midway between Vicky and Warren.

She let out a screech. "What's happened? I'm hideous."

"Looks like an improvement to me," said Lexi.

"You fool," shouted Veronica. "Crossing

dimensions during our powers – don't you remember the last time? They'll return soon, though. In the meantime, Apocalytes, get that idiot back through the portal and find us the boy. We will have our Apocalypse tonight. Wait… Where's Cruul gone?"

Everyone looked around, but there was no sign of Cruul anywhere.

Though they wouldn't have to look much farther for Milo. Suddenly two zorbs rolled into the clearing, coming to a gentle stop next to the Horsewomen. Attached all around them were what at first sight looked like little shoeboxes.

"What are they?" asked Veronica.

Bruiser took it upon himself to examine the nearest zorb. "There's loads of colored wires sticking out," he said. "And a timer."

"It's the leftover dung bombs," said Karen. "But who—"

A small boy with cornrows in his hair pulled up on a quad bike.

"IIIIII'm baaaaaaaaacck!" hollered Milo.

"It's the boy!" cried Veronica. "Get him!"

"Now, Milo!" I shouted, pulling Steve and Lexi to the ground.

Milo gave me a salute, before pulling a trigger from his pocket. He gave it a squeeze.

BOOM! BOOM! BOOM! BOOM! BOOM! BOOM! BOOM!

Animal droppings exploded everywhere, blinding Horsewomen and Apocalytes alike. The smell was horrific. As much as I could have watched the Horsewomen stagger around covered in dung all day, we didn't have much time.

"Lexi, we have to go," I said, pulling her up.

"Argh!" she yelped. "It hurts when I move too fast."

"Hang on," said Steve. He held his fingers to his mouth and made a piercing whistle. Just as I was about to ask him what he was doing, there she was. Polly the pony – wearing what looked like battle armor – burst through the portal, charging straight for us. Steve and I quickly lifted Lexi onto Polly's back. Steve then climbed up in front of her. As Polly galloped away, Milo pulled up alongside me on his quad.

"You took your time," I said as I hopped on behind him.

"I had to go back to the cave to raid the storage boxes," he said as the bike shot forward. "Did you like my 'I'm back' line, by the way?"

"Actually Veronica kind of used that already," I said.

"Really? Aw, man. I was going to say 'Did you miss me?'" he said.

"She used that one too," I said.

"Ugh. Veronica was always the worst. Don't worry, by the way, I removed the bomb from this bike."

I hadn't been worried. I was now. "Bomb?" I shouted.

"Yeah," said Milo. "They didn't know which bike Lexi would pick, so they put bombs on both of them. Obviously they only triggered the device on the bike she was on, but they didn't bother removing it from this one."

"Where are we going?" shouted Steve as we pulled alongside Polly.

"To the plane!" Milo yelled back. "Follow us."

Lexi let out a long groan. "Not another plane!"

We sped through the jungle with Polly close on our heels. The sky was black with clouds as the rain continued to pour down heavier than ever. In the distance the volcano was starting to crumble in on itself. Large cracks were already forming in the jungle floor. Just as Veronica had said, it looked like the island was imploding. I kept glancing over my shoulder, expecting to see the Horsewomen right behind us. But all I saw was the ground ripping apart, swallowing up trees and plants in the process.

"This is good," said Milo. "Sort of. It's going to make it much harder for them to catch up."

My heart leaped when we finally saw the plane. We burst out of the jungle and onto the long stretch of grass.

"Can you fly a plane?" I asked Milo.

"I've got a flight simulator on my computer at home," he said.

Well, that was something.

"I've only ever played it once, though," he added. "And I crashed my plane into the sea."

It was still better than nothing.

We pulled up alongside the plane. Milo and I jumped off the bike and helped Lexi down from Polly.

I rushed up the steps and pulled on the door. It swung open so quickly that I almost fell backward. Luckily Milo was behind me to catch me. What happened next wasn't so fortunate.

Agent Banks stepped out of the plane, pointing her gun at me.

"Of course," I groaned. "I should have guessed. You're in on it too."

"Down the steps," she said. "Move!"

"All right," I said. The four of us walked back down the steps.

"You going to shoot us?" asked Lexi.

"Please don't," said Steve. "I've been fighting

seven-headed dogs and eight-legged cats for months now. I'd hate to just get shot after all that."

"We're going to wait for my mistresses to get here," said Agent Banks, "I think they'll be very pleased with me. In the meantime you probably deserve an explanation."

"Please, no," I said.

"What?" she said.

"No more explanations," said Lexi.

"But..."

"Look," I said. "I'm sure your story is really fascinating. It's just that I swear if I hear another bad guy tell me all about their clever plans today my head is going to explode. Can we just assume that you were recruited by the Horsewomen, you infiltrated the **AIA** and then Cruul got you to send us on the show so he could trick us into opening the portal to bring back the Horsewomen. Is that fair to say?"

"Well... Yes, kind of..." she said, sounding deflated.

"Yeah, it's getting pretty old hat now with you all," said Lexi.

"But… But … don't you want to hear *why* I'm helping the Horsewomen?" she asked.

"A hundred pounds says it has something to do with acting," I said.

"Oh, for crying out loud," moaned Agent Banks. "Did Nigel tell you this? We'll be having words when I see him. It doesn't matter, though. All that matters is that I stopped you getting away. It was only when my imbecile of a partner told me he had given you the Time-Out device that I knew I had to come here personally."

"So you didn't get my messages?" I said.

"Sure, I did," she said. "I personally cut them out of the transmission so Speed never got a single one."

"Agent Speed wasn't involved in this, then?" I said, grateful to discover that at least someone on the planet wasn't.

"Speed?" she said. "Ha! That boy scout? Not a chance. You know he even managed to mess up handing out the parachutes. I gave him very clear instructions on which one you were meant to get – I fobbed him off with a story about them being calibrated for weight. But the idiot still ended up giving the bad one to Milo instead of you."

"Bad one?" asked Lexi.

"Yeah, I had it fitted with a device to affect its movement," she said. "Cruul was supposed to save Sam to look good to the public. Luckily Milo worked just as well. But then Speed messed up again, giving you that device. Fortunately on the flight here I was able to get in touch with Karen so they could neutralize its effects."

Milo nodded. "So that's why we couldn't disable the drone on the volcano."

"Exactly. But in a way I'm glad he gave you it because now I'm here and sure to get all the glory and praise from my mistresses for stopping you getting away. And I get to be here with them for the Apocalypse. This is the best thing—"

Without warning, Agent Banks dropped to the ground. She was out cold.

Milo leaned over her and, with a small tug, pulled something from her neck. He held it up. It was a dart, like the ones from the tranquilizer gun.

"Found some extra boxes of darts when I was looking for some robes that actually fit," said Zizi, carrying Pierre under her arm and spinning a dart gun around her finger as she walked toward us.

CHAPTER THIRTY-SIX

AIA

APOCALYPSE INTELLIGENCE AGENCY

"Zizi?" I said.

"Actually, no," she said, flashing an ID badge. "My real name is Callie Perkins. I'm an agent with the **AIA**. I was recently transferred from MI5, where I've been working deep cover for the past few years as a vacuous reality TV star, to investigate a suspected mole within the agency. Agent Banks here was working for the other side. All because she wanted—"

"To be an actor," I interrupted. "Yes, we know. But how—"

"I'll explain everything later," she said, kneeling to handcuff the unconscious Agent Banks. She pointed across the field. "Right now we have four very angry Horsewomen and a horde of fanatics in bathrobes on our tails. I'd say it's time we get ourselves out of here. Milo, help Lexi up those steps. Sam, help me carry Banks. You there, get that pony on the plane. Now!"

None of us were in a position to argue so we did as we were told.

After dumping Agent Banks into a seat, Agent Perkins headed straight to the captain's seat where she immediately started flicking switches. Pierre jumped into the copilot's seat beside her.

"Can you actually fly this thing?" I asked.

Agent Perkins grinned. "Didn't you see me win Who Wants to Be a Fighter Pilot?"

"No," I admitted.

She made a tutting sound. "You really should watch more reality TV," she said. "You might learn something."

"Er … guys," said Milo. "You might want to speed things up. They're almost here."

I looked out of the window. He was right. The Horsewomen were already close enough that I could see the looks of fury on their faces.

Suddenly the engines kicked into life.

"That's more like it," said Agent Perkins. "Now strap yourselves in, this could get bumpy."

The plane started to roll across the field but not nearly fast enough for my liking.

"Sam, look!" shouted Lexi.

I turned back toward the window. The Horsewomen were thundering toward us.

"Go faster!" I yelled.

"I'm trying," said Agent Perkins.

As the plane picked up speed, a pale-green horse

appeared alongside us, galloping faster than any horse I had ever seen. Veronica. The others weren't far behind.

"Can those things still fly?" asked Lexi.

"Doesn't look like it," said Milo as the plane pulled up, finally leaving the ground. The horses continued to thunder across the field below.

The ground itself began to crumble, but the four were relentless, their horses leaping and bounding their way over cracks and fissures that were filling with lava.

I saw Veronica look up, her rage burning hotter than the molten rock around her. She closed her eyes. And then she vanished, along with the others.

Three of them appeared next to me, dripping wet from the rain and incandescent with rage. And exhausted – each of them taking large breaths. The teleportation seemed to have drained them considerably.

They were looking around as though they had lost something.

"Where's Vicky?" asked Veronica.

Suddenly there was a banging at the cabin door. A desperate-looking Vicky was hanging on to it. "Let me in," she mouthed through the window.

Valerie hurried over to the door and started pulling at the handle.

"It won't open," said Milo calmly. "Not while we're in flight. It's the way they're designed."

"Ugh, I hate health and safety. Well, we'll see about that," said Valerie. She pointed a finger at the door, but nothing happened.

"You don't have the strength," said Violet.

But Valerie was determined. She gave a giant roar, then dropped to her knees in exhaustion as the door swung open.

But it didn't quite go to plan. Still attached to the door, Vicky smacked into the side of the plane, lost her grip and tumbled back toward the island.

Valerie had barely processed what had happened before Steve charged into her, sending her flying out of the plane after Vicky.

Violet screamed and waved her hand, flinging Steve all the way down the plane, his sword clattering to the ground. But the gesture weakened her, forcing her to grab on to the back of a seat just to stay upright. Suddenly Lexi was standing in front of her. Violet waved her hand again, but nothing happened. She was out of juice.

Enraged, she decided to throw a punch instead. That was a mistake. Lexi held up her good arm, grabbed Violet's, then twisted her hips, judo-tossing Violet out of the plane.

"I'm surrounded by idiots," said Veronica. With a wave of her hand, she knocked Lexi into a seat, at which point the seat belt strapped her in. She did the same to Milo and Steve, who had just clambered back to his feet. Then she turned to me.

"That's two Apocalypses you've ruined now," she hissed.

"Sorry about that," I said, edging backward.

"You will be," she said, taking a step toward me. Her foot made a clanging sound as it struck something metallic. Steve's sword. She waved her hand at it, but when nothing happened she reached down and picked it up.

"It's over," I said.

"For you, yes," she said, pointing the blade toward me. "I'm going to enjoy this."

I took another step back, then remembered something. "But you can't kill humans," I said. "Not directly. It's an ancient law."

She smiled menacingly. "Maybe," she said. "But there's nothing to say we can't hurt you. A lot. And when I'm done, *he* can finish you once and for all."

She pointed behind me. I turned around just in time to see Cruul crawling out of a hatch in the floor.

"My mistress," he said. "I'm here to help."

"No he's not," groaned Milo. "He obviously just stowed away in the hold, trying to escape. He probably snuck in when Banks was pointing her gun at us."

"I… No… I was… This was a … tactical maneuver," said Cruul. "Yes, that's it!"

"Whatever, Cruul." Veronica sighed. "Just grab him."

"As you command," said Cruul, smiling that smug smile of his.

I swiveled my head back and forth as Veronica and Cruul approached from either side. I eyed the open cabin door. There was only one move left to make. I could see no other way.

I grabbed on to the nearest seat with one hand, then, with the other, I reached into my hair and pressed the button on the Time-Out device.

The plane instantly plunged into darkness and began to dip. Amid screams from Lexi and whinnies from Polly, Cruul lost his balance, stumbling past me and colliding with Veronica, narrowly avoiding impaling himself on Steve's sword. The two of them slid down the plane toward the open door. At the last moment Veronica managed to stab the sword into the floor, bringing herself to a halt. As he slid through the door, Cruul grabbed hold of her ankles, dangling halfway out of the plane.

"Get off me, you fool!" she screamed as she kicked at his head. But Cruul wouldn't let go.

The cockpit door opened and out rushed copilot Pierre, going straight for Veronica's ankle.

"Get away!" shouted Cruul. His nose started to twitch.

A... A... A...

Achoooo!!!

The force of the sneeze was enough to loosen Cruul's grip. He was gone in an instant. Pierre, meanwhile, continued to bite at Veronica's leg.

"Shoo, you horrible mutt!" shouted Veronica. She waved her free hand, but nothing happened. Her powers were still spent. There was a clear look of panic on her face.

Steve whistled, causing Polly to charge toward her.

"No, wait, don't!" pleaded Veronica.

I swear there was a glint in the pony's eyes as she swung around and then bucked, sending a well-placed kick that booted Veronica through the cabin door. With some effort I slammed it shut and watched her fall back to what was left of the island.

Fin Del Mundo was shrinking, like a balloon

having the air let out of it. Seconds later it disappeared completely. The portal had claimed the entire island, just as Veronica had said.

Unfortunately there was still one other thing to deal with – the minor issue of the plane having no power. I rushed to the cockpit where Agent Perkins was sitting at the controls.

"Did Pierre sort out that horrible girl?" she asked.

"Yes, but…"

"Oh, good boy," she said as Pierre hopped back into the copilot's seat. "Someone's going to get an extra-special treat when we get home."

"But Zizi… I mean, Agent Perkins," I said. "We have no power."

"Oh, that," she said casually as the plane continued to tilt forward. "I wouldn't worry. The effects of a standard issue Time-Out only last for one minute and fifty-seven seconds."

We were now in a full-on dive toward the sea. I could hear screams from the cabin. Yet Agent Perkins looked completely calm.

"Are you sure?" I asked.

"One hundred percent," she said. "Well, maybe ninety. At a push … eighty-five."

The plane was hurtling toward the water. I could see the sharks circling.

And then the lights came back on.

"There we are," said Agent Perkins, effortlessly pulling us out of our nosedive at the last second. "Oh, look, the weather's clearing up now."

She was right. Like the island, the black clouds had all vanished.

"Looks like it's going to be a lovely day," she said.

CHAPTER THIRTY-SEVEN

AIA

APOCALYPSE INTELLIGENCE AGENCY

"This must be it," I said as Lexi, Milo and I walked down a long wood-paneled corridor with a single door at the end. When we reached the door, I knocked, and it swung open, revealing a rather grand office. The carpet was a dark-green tartan, and on the walls were paintings of serious-looking men and women. A good chunk of the room was taken up by a large antique oak desk, behind which sat the woman I had come to see.

"Hey, guys, come in." Even after seven days, the sight of Zizi in a black suit was still hard to wrap my head around.

"How are you all?" she asked.

"Good," we replied.

"Sorry about the hair, Sam," she said, giving me a sympathetic look.

I frowned, putting up a hand to cover the bald patch on the back of my head from when the **AIA** had removed the Time-Out device. That tape really was strong.

She took a sip of coffee and turned to Lexi. "How's the arm?" she asked.

"Getting better," she replied. "Going to miss the Judo World Championships, though."

Lexi didn't seem particularly sad about that, but Agent Perkins offered her commiserations anyway. "That's too bad," she said. "And I hear you're planning on cutting back the number of sports you're doing. Sounds like a sensible plan."

She turned to Milo. "And you've officially quit the band?" she said. "A lot of young girls are very sad right now. Although since Steve's to be your replacement, I'm sure they'll be OK. People seem to be buying our cover story that he's secretly been in a coma since the Hyde Park Incident, so that's good."

"Yeah," said Milo. "And Polly is going to feature in their next video."

"Well, thank you for agreeing to see me," she said. "I promised to explain everything. So if you've got questions, now's the time to ask them."

The first question that came to mind was the thing that had annoyed me the most. "If you thought Agent Banks might be bad, how come you still let her go ahead with sending the three of us to the island?"

Agent Perkins nodded. "The operation was under Banks's control, but some within the agency suspected she was dirty," she said. "Yet without proof, there was no way they could get the authorization from above to shut her down. I was sent in as part of a top secret parallel mission, of which Banks had no knowledge. The hope was she'd either make a mistake and reveal herself or I could find someone involved willing to flip on her. That's why I talked my way into joining the Apocalytes. That and to maintain the secondary objective for sending me on the show – ensuring that there was at least one **AIA** agent looking out for you."

"Looking out for us?" I said. "I don't remember seeing you doing much to save Lexi from those alligators."

"I was about to go for the gun before Cruul beat me to it," she said defensively. "I suspect Lexi would have found a way out of that situation herself, anyway. She's remarkably resourceful."

Lexi beamed at this.

"Any other questions?" said Agent Perkins, grinning back.

"Are they gone?" I asked. "For good?"

Agent Perkins' smile faded. "We don't know," she said. "From what we understand, the island and everyone on it disappeared through the portal. It's likely that they're back in the darkest dimension. But they escaped from there once. We can't rule out them escaping again. They also talked about new powers they had picked up. We obviously didn't see them at full strength this time, but we need to think about the possibility that one day we might. Which is actually something I wanted to talk to you three about."

"Us?" I said.

"Well, as you might have gathered from my office, my work on Fin Del Mundo and the job opening created by the sudden departure of Agent Banks has earned me a promotion. I've been given the task of assembling a brand-new team. Agent Speed will be joining me. And I was hoping you guys would too."

Lexi, Milo and I exchanged confused looks. "Sorry, what?" said Milo.

"We're not planning on sitting around waiting for the Horsewomen to show up again," she said defiantly. "If they're still out there, we're going after them. And who better to do that than the only people to have defeated them twice?"

I couldn't believe what she was asking. "That's funny," I said. "Because on both occasions, instead of telling people that we defeated them, you guys covered the whole thing up. All those news reports of most of the cast and crew from **End Games** going missing in the Bermuda Triangle?"

"Well, to be fair that is pretty much what happened," said Agent Perkins.

"It leaves out the bit about the return of the Four Horsewomen of the Apocalypse, though," I said.

Agent Perkins stared at me for a few seconds. "OK," she said at last. "I see what the issue is."

"Oh, you do?"

"Sure," she said. "You want recognition for what you've done."

"Yeah," I said. "That would be nice."

"Well, that's not how it works," she said. "For years I pretended to be a complete airhead. But I saved lives. You know why? Because when people dismiss you, they underestimate you. And when people underestimate you, they hand you the advantage. That's what Cruul did. He thought he knew how people worked, how they could be manipulated. He even thought he could tear you and Milo apart, but he underestimated your friendship. And the Horsewomen have underestimated you from the very beginning and always will. That's why we need you, Sam. But if recognition is more important to you than saving the world, then you should go. Because the public will probably never know about what you've done."

I stood there for about a minute, taking in what she had said.

"What about school?" I asked.

"You'd still have to go, obviously," she replied.

"Would we get paid?" said Lexi.

"Well, a government salary, but yes," she said. "And you'd have the entire resources of the **AIA** at your disposal. Lexi, you'd receive elite combat training. Milo, you'd have access to technology decades before it hit the market. And Sam… Um… We get ten percent off at some shops, though you have to be employed for six months for that… It's all in the welcome pack. But anyway, are you guys in?"

"Obviously!" said Lexi.

"Of course," said Milo.

After Hyde Park, I'd wanted a normal life again, but I knew now that wasn't possible. Not while there was a chance the Horsewomen were still out there.

I let out a sigh.

"Which shops?" I asked.

ABOUT THE AUTHOR

TOM NICOLL has been writing since he was at school, where he enjoyed trying to fit in as much silliness to his essays as he could possibly get away with. When not writing, he enjoys playing video games (especially the ones where he gets beaten by kids half his age from all over the world). He is also a big comedy, TV and movie nerd. Tom lives just outside Edinburgh with his wife, daughter and a cat that thinks it's a dog.

ABOUT THE ILLUSTRATOR

DAVID O'CONNELL cannot sing, play a musical instrument or dance, so would never be in a boy band. In fact, it is far more likely that the Apocalypse will destroy the universe than it is that David will ever agree to sing in public. Luckily for everyone, he is a writer and illustrator, living in London and having fun working on brilliant books like this one.

JOIN **SAM, LEXI** AND **MILO** ON BOTH APOCALYPTIC ADVENTURES.